Eric and Dud's Football Bargain

Eric and Dud's Football Bargain

by C. Paul Jackson

Illustrated by
Ned Butterfield

HASTINGS HOUSE, PUBLISHERS
NEW YORK

Published simultaneously in Canada by
Saunders of Toronto, Ltd., Don Mills, Ontario
Library of Congress Catalogue Card Number: 72-4259

Library of Congress Cataloging in Publication Data
Jackson, Caary Paul, Date
    Eric and Dud's football bargain.

    SUMMARY: Enthusiastic but unskilled, Dud agrees to play foot-
ball in order to get his new all-star neighbor to join the local Small
Stuff League team.
    [1.   Football—Stories]   I.   Title.
PZ7.J1322Er   [Fic]   72-4259
ISBN 0-8038-1911-0

Printed in the United States of America

Contents

6 · CONTENTS

Lineups of Offense Unit, Defense Unit, and Reserves for twenty-five Packers allowed by Small Stuff Football League rules.

Defense Unit
Left end: Wilson Coppock
Left tackle: Ed Fischer
Right guard: Bill Wyatt
Right end: Matt Fernandez
Left linebacker: Abe Taylor
Middle linebacker: Al Dimarzio
Right linebacker: Fred Skinner
Left cornerback: Manny Dillon
Right cornerback: Dudley Benton
Weak safety: Hans Hausee
Strong safety: Dick Mann

Offense Unit
Split end: Paul Field
Left tackle: Doug Flinn
Left guard: Fred Skinner
Center: Al Dimarzio
Right guard: Neil Boerman
Right tackle: Ted Morrison
Tight end: Bob Burch
Quarterback: Eric Rogel
Left halfback: Pete Granger
Right halfback: Whitey Howell
Fullback: Dick Klock

Reserves:
Pete Sawyer · Bert Rackley · Ken Johnson · Lloyd Spink · Pudge Lane ·

CHAPTER ONE

This Is a Good Deal?

ERIC ROGEL and Dudley Benton came to the football field where the Packers held practice workouts. The Small Stuff Football League required full equipment of pants, pads, jersey and helmet for practices as well as games. Eric and Dudley wore green stockings with two horizontal gold stripes. Their pants were gold; the jerseys green with gold numerals on front and back. The helmets were green with a gold P on the front.

"Packer Green and Gold makes a swell looking uniform," Dudley said. He looked Eric up and down, shook his head and added, "On you. Guess there isn't any uniform could do much toward making me look like a football player!"

"You want to call the whole thing off?" Eric asked quickly. "It'd be the smartest thing to do!"

"Huh-uh." Dudley shook his head. "We made a deal."

Except for the Packer uniform, Eric and Dud Benton bore little similarity. Eric was tall for a twelve-year-old. His hair was almost the color of the numerals on his jersey; his eyes were a deep blue. There was a litheness about him, a smoothness of movement that testified to fine coordination.

Dud was nearly a head shorter. His ninety-seven pounds were distributed so that he appeared to be heavier than Eric though his friend outweighed him by five pounds. Dud's hair was a mousy brown; his eyes were warm and bright, though more murky than brown in color.

"Well, well! Dud Benton in *playing* gear!" Another boy called out to Dud. "How about that? You don't look right without a sweatshirt and water bucket, Dud!"

"Hi, Whitey." Dud Benton's tone held no enthusiasm. He looked up at Eric, and nodded toward the boy with very blond hair. "Whitey Howell, Eric Rogel," Dud said. "Whitey was Packer quarterback last year. Whitey is—"

Dud broke off, dodged around Eric and yelled, "Mine!"

A man across the field had kicked a football—a high spiraling punt. He was wearing a green sweatshirt with COACH lettered across it.

"Stay away!" Dud motioned while he took two steps forward, then to his right, then back left. "I've got Coach's punt!"

Suddenly it seemed that the football came alive. It slanted away, and rose wickedly as Dud leaped. It sailed more than a foot above his stretching hands. Whitey Howell started toward the descending oval, but it was Eric Rogel who caught the twisting spiral. Long fingers gripped the oval almost caressingly. Eric drew back his arm and whipped the football in a level, past-the-ear throwing motion. The ball bored through the air straight toward the man who had kicked it. Coach Keefer moved forward only two steps to catch the pass.

The coach eyed Eric. "You throw a fine pass," he called.

Awe was in Dud Benton's expression as he looked from Coach Keefer to Eric. "That pass covered at least thirty yards," Dud said. "Straight and on a line!"

"Anybody can throw a football, if he works at it."

"Yeah!" Dud regarded the taller boy. "I could work at it thirteen years and ninety-two days and never throw a pass like that! You know something? You just made a believer out of me! I kind of wondered if you stalled about coming out for the Packers because you weren't really all that good. But a guy who snags a punt like that and breezes back a thirty-yard beeline pass *has* to have something! It

would be a crime for the Packers not to have a guy who handles a football like that!"

Eric shook his head. "The crime'll be what you're going to suffer," he said. "Let me know after a couple of workouts how good a deal you made— that's if this Keefer is anything like coaches back home!"

All the boys out for the Packers were dressed and ready. In uniform it was hard to distinguish veteran players from newcomers. Coach Keefer lifted a whistle that hung from a thong around his neck and blew a short blast.

"Everybody spread out for warmup exercises," he said. "We will always warmup before workouts and games. We'll try to learn a lot of different drills to avoid monotony. Today I will demonstrate how to do each exercise and then we will go through the drills together. First is the Side Straddle Hop."

Keefer stood at attention, then counted aloud. "One!" He swung his arms over his head and touched hands, at the same time moving his feet sideward in a single jumping motion. "Two!" He jumped back to starting position. Following the Hop, Coach Keefer demonstrated other exercises, giving directions for each.

The Squat Thrust. Stand at attention. On count of "one" bend knees and squat with hands on the ground in front of feet. On "two" thrust legs back so the body straightens out. Return to squat position on "three" and stand erect on "four."

Alternate Toe Touch. Stand with hands on hips. Keep legs straight, bend and touch left foot with right hand. Come back to starting position, bend and touch right foot with left hand.

Next the coach demonstrated push-ups. Assume prone position, face down, hands on ground at each side. Lift body so that arms are straight. Lower body until chest all but touches the ground. Lift and lower.

The Trunk Twister. Stand with hands on hips, feet comfortably apart. Without moving the feet, twist body as far to the left as possible then as far to the right as possible.

Running Backwards. Maintaining balance is most important.

Duck Walk. Squat on heels with hands on hips, feet fifteen to eighteen inches apart. Walk without straightening.

Dud watched the coach. The exercises looked easy. What was all this about football being so tough?

"All right, we'll go through the drills together," Keefer said. "Twenty Side Straddle Hops first."

At the close of the hops, Dud grinned at Eric. "Nothing to it," Dud said.

But going through each drill fifteen or twenty times soon had Dud breathing rapidly. Perspiration began to soak the T-shirt under his jersey and he discovered muscles where he had not realized there were any. When the not-often-used muscles began to protest under the strain Dud was panting hard.

"We will always end with the Grass Drill," Keefer said. "Run in place and when I yell, 'Down!' dive forward and hit the grass. When I yell, 'Up!' come erect and run in place. All right, run!"

Dud honestly wondered if he would survive the grass drill. The third time he hit the ground, he thought how wonderful it would be just to lie there. Bits of dirt and dead grass sifted through the jersey neck and beneath his T-shirt.

"Up!" Keefer shouted. "Up, up! Knees high! Get 'em up like you were trying to bump your chin!"

Dud groaned. How could he have ever thought Coach Keefer was a good guy? But he was only carrying water last year. This Keefer was a fiend. Dud was sure that each foot weighed a hundred pounds as he tried to lift them high. He was wondering how long he could survive when the coach finally called a halt.

Eric eyed Dud and grinned wickedly. "Isn't this just peachy-dandy fun?" Eric said.

"How much warming up does a fellow need?" Dud groaned. "I'm hot enough now to melt an iceberg!"

"We haven't done anything yet," Eric said. "He's just about ready to dish out the real stuff. How about getting sensible and saving yourself a lot of grief?"

Dud marveled that Eric was breathing only a

little faster than normal. "A deal's a deal," he mumbled. He thought, it's a good thing the first practice is about over. I'm a wreck. Another few minutes and—"

"Everybody should be well-loosened," Coach Keefer's words interrupted Dud's thinking. "Now we'll get on with developing blocking and tackling techniques."

Dud stared in disbelief while the coach brought two stuffed tackling and blocking dummies from his car. What had changed Keefer into a slave-driving monster? Was he trying to knock everybody out the first practice? Dud sneaked a glance around. He saw no other boy who looked as beat as he felt. A corner of Eric's mouth lifted in a crooked little grin as he met Dud's gaze. Dud groaned silently, forced his sagging shoulders to square.

"You should all know several principles that are behind my coaching," Keefer said. "Every boy is expected to give the best he has to make the Packers play the best football they can. No boy who comes to practices and gives his best will ever be asked to turn in his equipment, and we will strictly obey the Small Stuff League rule that every boy in uniform is in the game at least four plays. I will try to remember that you are only boys and not overcoach or expect the perfection a college or pro coach expects. I firmly believe that any team will be only as good in the long run as the member of the team who is weakest at blocking and/or tackling."

Coach Keefer stopped speaking for a moment, then a grin flashed across his face as he went on.

"I have one peculiarity—superstition, if you like—that you will get to know. I always signal we are ready to start a workout by booting a punt."

The grin disappeared and the coach's gaze traveled over the group of boys. Dud wondered if he imagined that Keefer looked at him a little longer than others.

"About blocking and tackling: a team on offense cannot move the ball without good blocking," Keefer said. "Any defense that is going to contain the other team's offense must have good tackling. Now, we will play a unit on offense and a unit on defense. Some of you may play both ways. But whether you are playing defense or offense, you must know how to block and how to tackle.

"Suppose your offensive platoon has a pass intercepted, or there is a fumble—right away you change from offense to defense. So you need to know tackling technique. On the other hand, one of your gang on defense recovers a fumble in the air —he can run with it. Or a pass is intercepted. In the instant that possession of the ball changes to your team, you are on offense and you have to be able to block potential tacklers away from your ballcarrier!"

Coach Keefer looked over the group, motioned

to Eric and said, "You've done some blocking, son?"

Eric hesitated, nodded slowly and said, "Yes, sir."

"Good." Keefer set one of the dummies a few feet away. "Show us how to throw a block."

Again Eric hesitated, then asked, "A full-body block, shoulder block or what?"

Dud was sure the question surprised the coach. But Keefer barely glanced at Eric. "A body block," he answered.

Eric charged at the blocking dummy. He launched his body and banged the stuffed dummy a yard back. Eric did not sprawl to the ground. Instead he landed on his hands and feet, arched his body and crowded against the dummy in a crablike motion.

"Fine technique." Keefer nodded. "I hope the rest of you noted that he bore down on the dummy as though he was going to run through his man. He threw his body across the thighs of the tackler and drove hard. Then he built a bridge with his body to be sure the potential tackler could not reach over him and get at the ballcarrier."

The boys formed two lines, and took turns at charging the dummies. Dud's turn came. He tried to imitate the short, choppy steps Eric had used, but as he barged into the dummy he knew that his attempted block was as awkward as it felt. The dummy tipped down only a little; Dud shot through the air over it. His face plowed into the ground. He scrambled to his feet, spitting dirt and grass.

"Your charge was too high," Coach Keefer said. "A high charge gives your opponent opportunity to slip the block. Or he can hand-fight you and knock you into the path of your ballcarrier."

Dud trotted to the end of the line. He was full of misery. What a chump he was! He had no business out here with guys who knew what they were trying to do.

How had he ever got into such a crazy deal?

Suddenly he was recalling one of his talks with Eric Rogel, the boy who had come to live with his grandmother next door to the Bentons. They yakked about a lot of things, and one day Dud hit on the subject of the Packers—the team in the Small Stuff Football League whose players came from this part of town.

"You look like maybe you play football," Dud said.

After a space of time that might have been seven or eight seconds but seemed longer, Eric Rogel said, "I played some with our school team last year "

"You any good?"

Eric gave Dud a brief look. "I made the league All Star team," he said shortly. "But I was no All American. Let's cut out the football talk, huh?"

Dud had no intention of needling his new friend. But when they talked, sooner or later football came into the conversation.

Dud was never able to pinpoint what touched Eric off. Maybe it was his own fanatical loyalty to the Packers—the team for which he had been water boy and general flunkey last year. Whatever the reason, Eric finally flared out fiercely.

"Football is a rat race right from Mighty Mite league up through high school! Probably on through college and the pros! I don't want any part of *any* football team!"

"Aw, come off it! Kids *gotta* play football!"

"Not this kid!" Eric eyed Dud from head to toe. "With all that weight, you could be a guard or center or something. *You* carry on for your dear old Packers!"

Real workouts came after all permission cards were signed. Things were different for a player than they had been for water boy. Dud moved along in the line for another try at the dummy without really realizing what he had got himself into. I'm no athlete, he thought. I should have kept my big mouth shut. Even now he did not understand why he had made the 'deal' with Eric.

But somehow things had got around to where Eric had agreed to go out for the Packers if Dud did—and stay on the team until Dud quit. He knew now that Eric was banking on Dud not being able to last through the tough training workouts.

Dud was abruptly aware of a silence. The coach was waiting for him to take his second turn at that fiendish dummy. He did no better than his first try. He spat dead grass and dirt as he pulled himself erect.

"How's for coloring this deal a deep blue and spell it M-U-R-D-E-R?" Eric eyed Dud when he came again to the end of the line. "And call it a day as of now?"

Why not? Eric was right, this was plain murder for a fellow like Dud Benton. But an odd stubbornness that he did not know he possessed came into Dud. He pulled himself together, sighed and shook his head. But he thought:

This is a good deal?

CHAPTER TWO

Coach Keefer Wants to Know

DUD WONDERED if he could even just stand there and listen to Coach without falling flat on his face. He was bone tired. It was a real struggle to concentrate on Keefer's words.

"As blocking is the basic fundamental of offense," the coach began, "so the first fundamental of a sound defense is tackling. In order to become a good tackler, you must like contact—want to tackle. My college coach believed that tackling is twenty percent technique and eighty percent desire. Whether you have eighty percent desire or less, you can improve your tackling by knowing how and working and working and working at it."

The coach went on with tips on proper tackling form. Get position on the ballcarrier . . . . feet well apart for balance and readiness to shift laterally . . . . legs coiled ready to launch your tackle . . . . should be low and up in head-on-tackling . . . . any tackle that knocks the ballcarrier down is a good tackle. . . .

Keefer placed two dummies some three yards apart. Lines formed in front of each dummy. Dud. stood at the end of one line. A boy from each line alternately charged at a dummy. The coach stood a little back of and between the dummies. Eric hit a dummy hard and knocked it a yard back before it slammed to the ground firmly in his grasp.

"Good, clean tackle," Coach Keefer observed. "Good form."

Whitey Howell earned a word of praise. Other boys flung themselves at a dummy and heard either praise or constructive criticism.

It's as tough as blocking, Dud thought.

His turn came all too soon. He was determined that this time he would not charge too high. His shoulder plowed into the ground about the same time it hit the dummy. Dud almost turned a somersault and the stuffed demon was barely jarred.

"Keep trying," Keefer said. "You'll catch onto the knack."

I'm so rotten he doesn't even tell me what I do wrong, Dud thought. He was miserable. Tackling was not just as tough as blocking—it was worse!

Eric drove the dummy to the ground then came and stood behind Dud.

"You threw your tackle too soon," Eric said. "You go after a guy too low and he's a cinch to straight arm you flat on your face!"

Dud said nothing. Too high, too low! Huh!

When his turn came for a second try, Dud aimed at the middle of the dummy. He would show that stuffed fiend! He launched his body with all the strength he could bring into play—but his take-off was from the wrong foot. His head slammed into the dummy on an angle and he slid off it. Momentum carried his feet and legs around against the other dummy and knocked it over.

"Quote," Whitey Howell said. "Any tackle that knocks the ballcarrier down is a good tackle. Unquote. Great going, Dud. What you need is the old water bucket and you'd snag *both* of them!"

Dud lay motionless a moment. Half-dazed, discouragement flooded through him. Why try to kid himself? A dud was a dud—something that would never explode. Dud Benton was a dud for sure.

"What he *doesn't* need is some wise-guy making cracks!" Eric Rogel glared at Whitey Howell. He reached down and hooked a hand beneath Dud's arm. "You all right?" Eric asked.

"I'll be okay," Dud mumbled. "Tough to do, but I'll get it. Get the knack of blocking, too."

Eric's eyes held a puzzled expression. He

shrugged and said to nobody in particular, "How about a character like him?"

Dud misunderstood. He eyed Whitey, then Eric. "Maybe this is M-U-R-D-E-R," he said. "For sure I wouldn't color it red-white-and-blue-hurray! But I'm going to be back next practice—every practice. And so will you!"

Coach Keefer did not make a big thing of it. He spoke to Eric and Dud after he whistled the practice session to a close. "Like to talk to you fellows," he said in a low tone. "Only take a minute."

He's going to ask for my pads and uniform, Dud thought. But Coach had said that he never asked a boy to turn in his equipment. Keefer pulled two three-by-five cards from a pocket when he and the boys were alone.

"You left blank the space after Position Trying For," he said to Dud.

"Yes, sir. I—I—well, I don't know what I'm trying for!"

Keefer nodded, looked toward Eric. "You left that space blank and also Experience, Rogel."

"Yes, sir."

The coach waited, as though expecting some explanation. Eric said no more. After a moment or two, Keefer said, "I had a feeling before we came out here—perhaps because of the way you completed most of the card without question. Obviously the feeling was sound. You have filled out such cards before. You have played in an organized league—at least you have had coaching. Frankly, in ten years of coaching Small Stuff teams, I have never had a boy with greater potential."

Again Keefer seemed to be waiting for Eric to speak. Eric said nothing. Dud was surprised at the question the coach asked then. The manner in which Eric jerked his eyes to Keefer and stared showed that he was also surprised.

"Did you live in Texas before coming here, Rogel?"

Eric's stare became a frown. He said, "What's the difference where I lived?"

"You did live in Texas?"

"Yes."

Keefer nodded. "Rogel is not a real common name. And I recalled reading something about a Rogel playing football in Texas. I have no desire to pry. But aren't you from this same Texas family of football fame?"

"What if I am?" Eric's expression was defiant. "Okay, it's true! But I didn't want to ever play football again! I—I—"

Eric broke off. Dud saw Eric's eyes glisten as he blinked rapidly. He knew that Coach Keefer also saw that Eric was worked up emotionally. Keefer turned to Dud, shook his head and touched a finger to his lips. After a moment Eric swallowed hard and went on.

"My older brother, Bill, was the best football player our high school ever had," Eric said. "He was the best schoolboy passer in the state. In three years as quarterback Bill had only five passes intercepted. Now that he's in college, he'll probably make All-American."

Eric stopped a moment, shook his head a little before he went on.

"I suppose that no coach would have played me anywhere but quarterback when Bill had built such a fantastic record. It was okay with me at first —I got a charge from being in the same spot my brother had been when he played on his sixth grade team. Bill and I used to practice passing at home. He showed me how to grip the ball and how to develop a quick release. Bill never rode me. But Dad! You'd think I did something to disgrace the Rogels when I'd be intercepted in games!"

Two tears edged from beneath Eric's lids. He dashed a hand across his eyes. Dud realized that they were tears of frustration at the memory.

"I threw six interceptions in the game for the city championship," Eric continued. "And we lost. Six interceptions in one game—more than Bill threw in three years! Kids blamed me, said some real nasty things. And I could tell Dad was really ashamed. Even our coach as much as blamed me on a TV sports show. He said that no team could win when they had so many turnovers. I was sick of football. I never intended handling a football again!

"I was glad when Dad and Mom went to South America to set up a new operation for his company, and they sent me here to live with Gram for a year. It would be okay with me if they left him down there *more* than a year! I hope I never have to go back to Texas and their football-is-all-that-counts stuff!"

A silence held for what seemed to Dud a long time. Finally Coach Keefer said, "I think you were over-sensitive. I don't believe your coach was putting blame on you because your team lost the city championship. He was surely correct about turnovers being costly. I can see why you soured on football, though. What puzzles me is why you came out for our team."

Dud squirmed. "I guess I'm responsible," he said. He looked from Eric to the coach while he told of his needling Eric until the "deal" came about. "I didn't know about Eric's hassles," he finished. "Also, I didn't really expect to be so awful. I—I guess we'd better call off the whole thing and quit the Packers!"

Coach Keefer looked at Eric, then at Dud.

"If you want to release Rogel," he said quietly, "that is your privilege. And it will be his choice to stay with the team or not. As for you quitting because you are—ah—so awful, as you put it, don't do it."

Coach Keefer looked away across the practice field and his eyes held an odd light when he looked back at the boys.

"I told you fellows I always start a workout by booting a football," he said, "I didn't tell you why. It goes back to when I was 'awful' at kicking. My high school team needed a punter. I tried for the job. The very first effort, I dropped the football as the coach had showed, but too wide. My kicking foot missed it entirely and I landed on the back of my lap!"

Keefer chuckled, gave his head a little shake.

"All the guys laughed. I wanted to dig a hole and climb into it. But Coach told me that a fellow with my long legs could get the knack and make himself into a punter—if he would work at it."

Keep trying. You'll catch onto the knack. Words that the coach had said after his terrible tackle try came into Dud's thoughts. Coach Keefer eyed him soberly.

"I worked," he said. "And *worked,* and WORKED! One of the most satisfying things that ever happened to me came when I was given a football scholarship for four years at State U because of my ability to kick a football. That's why I open every practice with a punt—to remind myself that you can make yourself into about anything you want—by working and *working* and WORKING!"

The coach gave Eric a brief look.

"That's all," he said. "Thanks for staying and listening. And remember I never ask a boy to turn in his equipment. The only way to drop off my squad is to quit yourself."

CHAPTER THREE

A Few Facts of Life

DUD CHARGED at the tackling dummy. He launched his body off the right foot and slammed his shoulder against the instrument of torture. He drove the dummy a yard back in the clutch of his arms and was on top when it toppled.

"The way to tackle!" Coach Keefer nodded. "Fine form. That kind of tackle will stop the ball-carrier cold!"

Dud trotted to the end of the line. He felt a great satisfaction. Let's see: this was the third practice. Say he had averaged four blocking efforts each practice and four tackles. How about a dud earning Coach's praise in two dozen skirmishes with the stuffed monster? Not bad. Not bad at all.

He had caught some passes and he felt that he had not been really terrible in other drills Coach Keefer gave them. But this was the first time he had not plowed into the dirt, or hit so high that he shot over the thing, in blocking and tackling drill with the dummies.

Coach Keefer blew his whistle before Dud's turn came again. The coach said, "We will take part in the Small Stuff Jamboree next week. It's the first jamboree for the Small Stuff League. Each team will play two regular periods, against a different league team each period. Scrimmaging gives a coach a view of his player strength, but playing against members of your own squad, using the plays your team will use in regular games, you simply can't put out like you would against other fellows.

"So, the Jamboree will give coaches a look at their players under game conditions against guys who don't know the plays and what's coming. We have to get started on an offense and a defense pattern."

Dud glanced toward Eric. Dud had no doubt that his tall friend would be tabbed by Coach to play quarterback. He looked across at Whitey Howell. Dud was sure from Whitey's scowling expression that the Packer quarterback from last year also felt that he had lost his job. Eric's expression was hard to read.

Well, Dud thought, this is old stuff to Eric.

And he is not kidding about not wanting to play. He couldn't care less if Coach left him out entirely. Then that odd stubborn something came to the top of Dud's thinking again. But he's going to be playing for this team all season—if he waits for me to quit!

"There are almost as many offensive sets as there are players," Coach Keefer said. "Some of you no doubt would choose the Wishbone-T, the I formation, the Power-I, the Pro Set, or some other popular formation, if I gave you a choice. Now, let's concede right off the bat that *every* offensive formation, even the old single-wing and double-wing, has advantages."

Keefer waited a moment, seemed to be considering before he went on.

"However, I told you fellows I hoped not to over-coach. I doubt that your football experience —for the most part, surely—provides a base for fancy offensive sets. In my book, no matter what system of offense a team uses, blocking is the key to its success. The same goes in reverse for defense— evading the blocker and good solid tackling is the backbone of defensive play."

Again Coach Keefer stopped speaking. His gaze roved over the group.

"From things I have checked in practices so far, I think we have material for a good diversified offense. That means that we have a passer, receiver and blockers for a passing game—but we also need backs who can run and smash the line. We will run our offense from a basic T formation, with two half-backs and a fullback in the backfield with the quarterback."

He called off eleven names for the offense unit and told each boy the position he would play. Eric Rogel was at quarterback; Kip Ryskowski and Pete Granger at the halfback positions, and Dick Klock at fullback for the offensive backfield.

"Because I believe that you fellows can learn more quickly duties of the defense—and because I know this set better from my own experience—we are going to use the 4-3 defensive set. Actually, this defense is made up of four linemen, three linebackers, two cornerbacks and two safeties. We'll need work on it, of course. But I truly believe it is easier to play, and fully as effective if not more so, than a five or six man line with rover backs and so forth."

Dud was listening, but he admitted that the coach lost him in discussing the offense. But what was the difference? It was a cinch that Dud Benton would not be picked to play offense—oh, well, maybe in the line at guard or something, when Keefer had to keep the league rule of every-player-in-the-game-at-least-four-plays.

Then Dud was amazed—stunned—to hear his name called for right cornerback on the defensive team.

The coach spaced four boys for the first line of defense. He put left, middle and right linebackers about a yard behind the front four. Keefer placed Dud four yards wide of the right linebacker and about a yard and a half deeper. Manny Dillon was similarly placed behind the left linebacker on the opposite side. While the coach placed boys at the strong-side and weak-side safety positions, Dud called across in low tone to Dillon.

"What does a cornerback do?"

"I don't know for sure. The team I played for last year in the Smaller Stuff League used a six-man line, a rover back and four defensive backs." Dillon shrugged. "Cornerbacks tackle any ballcarrier who gets past the linebackers, I guess."

Coach Keefer came back from setting the safety men. "Except for kicking situations," he said, "the center snap is to the quarterback on all our plays. Potential pass receivers run their routes downfield when the play is a pass. The tight end mostly blocks, but he can also receive passes. We will have plays where he is the primary receiver and he can always be a secondary receiver.

"All backfield men and the split end—usually at the opposite side of the field from the tight end —are eligible to receive passes. Today, we are going to work on three basic plays: a drive off-tackle, a smash into the line over guard or center, and a play-action pass in which the quarterback has the option of passing or running the ball. It's called a rollout in some instances. Okay, we'll try them."

The offense unit walked through the plays. The coach worked with individual players on blocking assignments. Defensive players merely stood in position, making no effort to stop the ballcarrier. After several walk-throughs, Keefer had the offense run the plays at moderate speed. The defense still were not allowed to stop the ballcarriers.

They may be basic plays, Dud thought, but the defense will clobber them when we can tackle.

"Okay," Coach Keefer said. "We'll scrimmage. Run the plays like you were in a game, Rogel. Let's see how you fellows have absorbed blocking technique. You defensive men—show ballcarriers some tough tackling!"

In the next few minutes Dud Benton learned there were vast differences in watching an offense run plays in dummy scrimmage and going against the offensive plays when blockers were going all-out to clear the way for ballcarriers.

Al Dimarzio snapped the ball to Eric Rogel. Eric took two backward steps as though he was going to pass. Dud looked around without being really conscious that he was searching for a pass receiver. He jerked his gaze back to Eric just in time to see the quarterback had faked a pass, and slipped the ball to Pete Granger. Granger roared into a hole off-tackle on Dud's side. Dud took one step toward the ballcarrier—and was hit by a jarring block thrown by Dimarzio.

Pete Granger might have gone all the way after he shot past the tangle of Dimarzio and Dud, except that Keefer blew his whistle to kill the play.

"A good block!" Coach Keefer inclined his head toward Al Dimarzio. "Shows you that down-field blocking pays off." Then to Dud: "You use your hands on defense, Benton! You can't just stand there and let a blocker mow you down. Use your hands, shove him down!"

Dud tried to 'shove' blockers down. He failed miserably.

He was shunted aside by a brush block when Eric called a pass—and tight end Bob Burch grabbed a short pass from Eric and rambled for twenty yards. Then Eric faked a handoff, faked a pass, cut through the line and bore down on Dud. Dud used his hands trying to stave off a block, was only partially successful, and ground his face into the turf when Eric straight-armed him hard.

Dud Benton began to wonder if the scrimmage would ever end. He was knocked down, trampled, shoved aside every play, whether the ballcarrier came to his side or not. Finally—was it minutes or hours?—Keefer blew his whistle and said, "That's all for today. We'll scrimmage again tomorrow. We are a long way from ready to meet any other team in the jamboree."

Dud could not suppress a groan as he strad-dled his bike. Eric surveyed the chunky lad, and said sourly, "Are you ever going to get conscious?

Can't you see that you're only being used for cannon fodder while Keefer sharpens his offense? Only time you'll ever get into a game is when we're ahead—or so far behind in the last quarter it doesn't matter—and then only because of the rule that every guy has to—"

Eric broke off, kicked at the ground before climbing on his own bike.

"Skip it," he said. "I shouldn't lip off, but—oh, nuts! You may have learned some football facts of life today, and for sure you're going to learn plenty more!"

CHAPTER FOUR

Small Stuff Jamboree

ERIC WAS nowhere in sight when Dud wheeled his bicycle from the garage. Eric's bike was not in his grandmother's garage next door. Well, he's probably gone on ahead, Dud told himself. Maybe Coach wanted to see him before the Jamboree began, or something.

Try as he might to rationalize as he pedaled toward City Park, Dud could not keep from feeling uneasy. Eric must have known that even if he had to leave early, Dud would still have gone with him. Eric couldn't be mad, could he? Okay, so he spit out that Dud was stupid not to see that he was cannon fodder, that Coach would play him only when he had to. That was two practices ago—and Eric had been sorry. He said—

"Hey, hold up a sec, Dud!"

The call came from a boy in Packer uniform riding a bicycle in the street that ran into Park Avenue. Dud swerved a little to make room for Whitey Howell to ride beside him, and said, "Hi, Whitey."

After all, a fellow couldn't try to kid himself. Dud went on with his thoughts. The main thing in this whole deal is to keep Eric Rogel sparking the Packer offense—not to make a football player out of Dud Benton.

"Where's your wonder-boy pal?" Whitey asked.

The words did not immediately register with Dud. It was more the way Whitey said them. "I guess you mean Eric," Dud said after a moment. "He'd left when I came out. What's with the sarcastic tone?"

"Why wouldn't I be sarcastic! This All American character comes in and takes over—and you dog it when he runs offense to make him look better than he is!"

Dud almost ran his bike into the curb as he jerked his startled gaze to the white-haired boy. Whitey Howell had lost his job as quarterback to Eric, but—

"Don't look as though you never heard of dogging!" Howell interrupted Dud's thought. "You stood around and let Rogel parade past you! Then when Coach gave me a chance to run the offense, you clobbered the same play!"

Dud was honestly puzzled. Dogging? *Me!* Gosh, I'm trying to do the best I can all the time. I wouldn't know how to dog it!

Then he remembered that during scrimmage yesterday, he managed to avoid a block Dimarzio threw at him and tackled Howell. Well, more like knocked him enough off balance that the safety man rushed in and drove him to the ground. A warm glow suddenly filled Dud.

How about that? The question exploded in his brain. He barely saved his bike from careening into the curb with a last second swerve. *Whitey Howell accuses me of letting Eric go, but clobbering him! Wow! He must think I can really play football!*

He said aloud, "You've flipped, Whitey. You couldn't be any farther out!"

They were at City Park. Whitey Howell scowled while he lowered his bike's kick stand. "Nuts!" He said. "You can't squirm out of it. I'll get even with you—and Rogel, too!"

The Packer offense unit spread over their end of the football field to receive the kickoff from the Cowboys. Eric Rogel and Pete Granger were the deep men. Dick Klock and Whitey Howell were ten yards in front of the back pair.

The Cowboy kick was high and five yards short of the goal line. Eric yelled, "Mine!"

Eric waited and was running full stride when he fielded the kick. Pete Granger knocked the first defensive man down under the kick wide. Eric swung past the tangle of Granger and the Cowboy, sped straight upfield, then cut sharply toward the left sideline.

Packer reserves and players of the defensive platoon stood before their bench, yelling and screeching wildly. Eric was in the clear! He would go all the way into the end zone. He had only to get past one man—the kicker—to run the kickoff back for a touchdown.

Then Dud joined in the descending groan from Packer supporters in the stands. The last Cowboy shoved aside a weak blocking attempt of Whitey Howell. Eric was driven out of bounds just over the Cowboy forty-yard line.

How about that runback? Dud asked himself, and got an answer as though his question was aloud.

"Beautiful!" Al Dimarzio clapped the boy next to him on the back. "That Rogel can fly! He can do it all! Now, we go to work!"

Dimarzio ran out to replace the boy Coach Keefer had put in just to receive—he was a good blocker and a little faster than big Al Dimarzio. The offense unit broke from the huddle. Eric crouched behind the broad posterior of Dimarzio. Eric called, "Seventy-two! Twenty-six! Twelve! Hut! Hut! Hut!"

Dimarzio snapped the ball on the second "Hut!" Pete Granger slanted across from left halfback, took Eric's handoff and slashed off-tackle for five yards. The referee called, "Second and five!"

Dick Klock smashed into the center of the line. Three yards. Eric was establishing the running game, Dud thought. Football people go on about third down and short yardage being a passing situation for smart quarter-backs. What'll Eric do? Maybe a deep pass?

Eric Rogel took the snap, went back two steps, faked a handoff to Howell crossing from right halfback. Then Eric dashed into a hole between guard and tackle, faked a defensive back with a fine head feint and drove at the Cowboy safety man.

The defensive man refused to scare and dropped the Packer quarterback at the Cowboy twenty-six. It required six plays to move the ball into the end zone.

Granger carried on a sweep to the strong side, to the twenty-four. What seemed to be another sweep turned into a reverse after Eric faked a handoff to Granger, pivoted and flipped the ball to Whitey Howell. Eric slid behind the line and put a good block on the defensive end. It looked as though Howell would turn the corner and go for a touchdown. But the defensive back on that side recovered quickly from having initially gone the wrong way. He dropped Howell on the eighteen.

A bunched defense stopped Klock at the line

of scrimmage. Fourth down, two yards for a first down, sixteen to a touchdown. Coach Keefer sent Kip Ryskowski out to replace Howell. "Tell Rogel to run a quarterback keep," the coach said. "Block for him!"

Eric faked a handoff to Klock so well that Dud's heart leaped into his throat, thinking that Eric had disregarded the play Coach sent in. Then as the Cowboy defense ganged the middle to stop Klock, Dud saw the ball held behind Eric's hip as he sneaked along behind the line. Everybody in the Cowboy secondary had been fooled as badly as Dud Benton—except their safety man.

Eric slanted toward the red flag on the sideline at the goal line. But the safety man drove him out of bounds two yards short of the double chalk mark.

Burly Dick Klock smashed into the line. One yard. He seemed to be cracking over guard the next play. But Eric put the ball into the fullback's midriff, brought it out and pitched a lateral out to Ryskowski in the flat zone. Ryskowski hurried into the end zone without a hand being laid on him.

Eric carried for the point after touchdown. He crossed the goal line by swinging wide and just plain outrunning Cowboy defenders. Packers, 7; Cowboys, 0.

"Is that Rogel something, or is he something!" Manny Dillon whacked Dud on the back. Dud nodded. "Now all we have to do is show the Cowboys we have a defense as tough as our offense," Manny said. "Nothing to it!"

The Cowboys soon gave evidence that they had never heard of Dillon's nothing-to-it. They received the kickoff that followed the Packer touchdown and ran the ball back to their forty-one yard line. Right off their quarterback established their running game.

A smash off their left tackle. Dud saw the ballcarrier break through the hole. He made ready to charge the Cowboy as though he was the tackling dummy. Only at the last instant did he see the blocker. Dud's fending hands were too late. The blocker crashed into him and Dud sprawled on the ground while the ballcarrier slashed upfield.

Twelve yard gain, first down.

That was the longest gain of the Cowboy drive. But they racked up first down after first down in a steady march upfield. Only once was Dud successful in avoiding his blocker—and the ballcarrier was slanting through Manny Dillon's territory that time.

Two seconds more than half the playing time of the Cowboy-Packer period showed on the scoreboard clock when the Cowboys pushed into the Packer end zone.

The point after touchdown was scored through Dud Benton's side. A crushing block obliterated Dud. As he pulled himself together and got to his feet, an odd thought flitted across the back of Dud's mind. He was learning more of the football facts of life, just as Eric had predicted.

Kicking away from Eric Rogel, the Cowboys stopped Pete Granger at the Packer twenty-nine on the kickoff after their touchdown. Then the Packer offense began to move again. Eric drove them to the Cowboy nineteen, but Howell fumbled a handoff on the next play and the Cowboys recovered the ball at their sixteen.

Now the powerful Cowboy ground attack pushed the Packers relentlessly toward the Packer end zone. Midfield. Packer forty. A first down at the twenty-two. Coach Keefer sent a replacement out from the bench: Whitey Howell, in at right cornerback for Dud Benton.

Inexplicably to Dud, the Cowboy quarterback left the attack that had been grinding down the Packers. He called a pass. The ball was poorly thrown, much too wide for the receiver to reach. Whitey Howell cut across and grabbed the pass. His interception halted the Cowboy drive.

Time ran out before Eric Rogel could get the Packer offense moving. As the Packers trotted off the field, Dud asked Eric, "Why did they pass? They were killing us on the ground."

"Sometimes a quarterback figures that a sub coming into the defense cold won't be quite organized," Eric said. "Easy meat for a pass into his area. Or it could have been their coach sending in a play aimed at the substitute. Sometimes the best strategy backfires in this crazy game!"

After a Bears-Rams jamboree period of play the Packers took the field against the Falcons. Coach Keefer started Whitey Howell at quarterback. Eric Rogel was shifted to free safety in the defensive platoon.

Neither team threatened seriously to score until the scoreboard clock showed twenty-nine seconds left to play.

Howell called a pass and Falcon linemen pressured him hard. He aimed the ball toward Paul Field, but the throw was off target. A defensive back intercepted and ran the ball back to the Packer seventeen.

Coach Keefer kept Eric in the free safety position and moved Whitey Howell to right cornerback. Dud watched Eric when it was clear the Falcons were going to pass. Did he imagine that Eric loafed as he drifted casually to cover a potential receiver running a deep pattern? The ball was thrown to a back running a sideline route; overthrown and out of bounds. The incomplete pass stopped the clock.

Seven seconds left. Time for one play. The Falcons did not line up in formation for a field goal try. Well, heck, Dud thought, there aren't many field goal kickers in the Small Stuff League. It has to be a pass.

The same Falcon who had been wide open the play before ran deep past Howell toward Eric. But Eric had him covered. Then the Falcon put on a burst of speed and was suddenly past Eric. He stood all alone in the end zone. All that was needed for a Falcon touchdown was for the passer to get the ball to him. And the ball was boring through the air straight for the receiver.

It seemed that Eric came alive at the last instant. His lunging leap was almost too late, but he managed to tip the ball just enough to spin it out of the receiver's reach.

Incomplete pass. Time was up. Packers, o; Falcons, o.

Dud said nothing when Eric came off the field, just eyed him. Finally Eric moved irritably. "Go on, say what you're thinking—that I was maybe dogging it out there to discourage Keefer from playing me on defense, I suppose!"

"You said that, Eric. I didn't!"

"Okay." Eric shrugged. "Maybe the idea came to me. But I wasn't dogging it. I loafed deliberately going out for that guy on the sideline pass. I figured he'd go back and tell his quarterback he could beat me, and they would put the ball into the air my way."

Eric stopped a moment. Dud stared, nearly open-mouthed. There sure was a lot to be learned about defensive play. Inside stuff. Eric misinterpreted Dud's expression.

"Okay, so think what you want!" Eric flared. "Turned out the guy was faster than I thought and he nearly made me look bad. That's the way this crazy game goes.

"When are you going to wise up and chuck the whole business?"

Dud said solemnly, "I'm not. Only thing I hope is that I can learn half as much about playing as you."

Eric gave him a look, mumbled, "Nuts!", and headed toward the bicycle racks.

CHAPTER FIVE

It's Done with Mirrors

ERIC CAME OUT while Dud was pouring gasoline into the tank of the Bentons' power mower. "Fine thing to do to a pal," Eric said. "Grandma saw you out here and reminded me that her grass could stand cutting."

"Grass doesn't care when it grows around here." Dud matched Eric's light tone. "A little rain and it will need cutting again in a week or so."

"Yeah." Eric hesitated, then said, "I was going to come over sometime this morning. I guess I owe you an explanation. You wonder why I went on ahead to the game. Well, I had to help Gram with some errands. Then she dropped me off afterward at City Park.

Dud said, "Gosh, you don't have to explain. I didn't—" He broke off and grinned a little ruefully. "I was going to say I didn't think anything about it, but I did. I wondered if you were sore at me, or something."

"No," Eric said, "you got it all wrong."

Coach Keefer called the squad together after Dimarzio led the warmup calisthenic drills. Dud felt good inside. He was breathing only a little faster than normal. Maybe he was not much of a football player, but at least the warmup drills were no longer agony.

"The Jamboree showed that we do some things well," Keefer began. "We showed weakness in others. I honestly believe we were a better team than the Falcons. We should have scored against them. On the other hand, the Cowboys made our defense look very bad. We'll work hard to improve *that!*"

The coach went on, pointing out mistakes, singling out plays boys had made that deserved praise. Finally he said, "I can't let myself off the hook as to mistakes. I have been making one in not trying to develop a place kicker. Point-after-touchdown tries are not going to be made consistently by passing or rushing.

"We need a kicker who can boot the ball through the goal post uprights and over the crossbar on conversions. Also, there could be times when a field goal from, say inside the fifteen yard line, would win a game."

Keefer's gaze traveled around the group.

"We're going to start today to develop a dependable place kicker," he went on. "Dimarzio, come with me. Any of you who thinks he can place kick, follow us. The rest of you take alternate cracks at blocking and tackling the dummies."

Eric nudged Dud. "Go with 'em," Eric said.

"You flipped your lid? I don't know anything about place kicking!"

"None of those guys do, either." Eric indicated the three boys who broke away. "If they did they would have been showing off before now. They're going along mostly to get out of hitting the dummies."

Dud just shook his head. Could be, he thought. But I need tackling practice.

"Go on, I dare you!" Eric eyed Dud. "You think football is so great—here's your chance to be a star winning a game in the last three or four seconds!"

Dud wondered afterward what made him suddenly decide to accept Eric's dare. Something about the way he talked? Some deep-down hope that Dud Benton just *might* have an ability he didn't know about? Whatever it was, Dud trotted after the group headed for the goal posts at the south end of the field.

"We had a fine place kicker when I did the punting for State U," Coach Keefer told the group of hopefuls. "There were five things he said every place kicker should do.

1. Kick in the same rhythm every time.
2. Kick from exactly seven yards behind the line of scrimmage. This is the ideal spot to keep linebackers from looping around the blockers and reaching the kicker.
3. The right foot should be a little in front of the left in the stance. Approach the ball in a straight line, a small step with the right foot, a big step with the left—then kick.
4. Keep his head down during the whole effort, even during the follow through. If he looks up he is likely to flub the kick.
5. Have confidence that the ball will go over the crossbar."

The coach tossed a football to Dimarzio, told him to pass the ball back, that he would be holder.

"Everything I've said applies only to right-footed straight kicking," Keefer said. "Any of you kick soccer style or left-footed?"

They were all right-footed kickers. The coach crouched on one knee, called, "Hut!", took Dimarzio's snapback and set the ball for each boy. Dud watched, kept repeating to himself: *small step with the right foot, big step with the left then kick . . .*

keep your head down . . . confidence that the ball will go over the bar.

Dud was the fourth to kick. He stood waiting for the coach's "Hut!", still repeating Keefer's former teammate's advice. He took the small step and the big one then his foot met the football squarely. The oval rose end-over-end, split the goal post uprights ten feet above the crossbar.

Surprise flooded through Dud. Keefer said, "Beautiful! That one had height and carry to have been good kicked from ten yards farther back!"

Then came the elation. Dud felt wonderful. And after kicking five more—two wide, one that did not rise enough and went under the bar, and two good kicks—Dud still felt warm and good. He'd boomed the ball every time, no flubs.

"You can be a good place kicker, Benton," Coach Keefer said. "Remember what my coach told me—work, WORK and *work!*. Practice kicking every chance you get."

Strangely Eric did not grumble, made no protest when Dud asked him to hold for him to kick. "I did it a little last year," Eric said. "Coach believed three guys play about equal parts in successful place kicks—the center making a snap the holder can grab without losing a fraction of a second, the holder placing the ball fast and the same every time, and the kicker."

"Dimarzio will work with us, I know," Dud

said. "But I ought to kick more than just when the team practices. How about us putting up a goal post back of our garage and you hold for me whenever we can get together?"

That was when they ran into protest. Neither Eric's Grandmother nor Dud's parents wanted a goal post in their yards. It was Eric who fastened a wire from the corner of the Benton garage across to a tree, exactly ten feet above the ground. They tied pieces of cloth 23 feet, 4 inches apart to mark the width between the uprights on a regulation goal post.

They practiced after school; they practiced Saturday; they practiced with Dimarzio after Packer workouts.

After one workout, Coach Keefer watched Dud kick four of five between the uprights. "Beautiful," the coach said. His eyes twinkled then and he added, "For a fellow who 'didn't really appreciate how awful' he'd be, I would say you've come a long way." He nodded. "Yes, a long way. Just might be you'll kick one tomorrow night to win the game!"

It may have been first game jitters; it could have been the defensive units of both Packers and Rams forced mistakes. Whatever it was, every scoring threat mounted by either team's offense was blunted by fumbles, intercepted passes, penalties or a turnover of the ball on a punt.

Dud lost some of the doubt he held about ever learning cornerback play when he stuck with a receiver so tightly that the Ram could not hold a pass that would have given his team a first down on the Packer nine.

In the next series of down, all his doubts were back.

He failed to turn a ballcarrier in on a sweep, missed the tackle, and the Rams would have had a touchdown except that the ballcarrier stepped out of bounds avoiding the safety man.

It came down to the final twenty seconds of playing time, a scoreless game; Packer ball, third down on the Ram seven, goal to go. Eric threw a pass that was snagged by Paul Field in the corner of the end zone—but the split end came down with both feet beyond the end line.

Incomplete pass. The play had used up nine seconds. Eleven seconds left to play, fourth down. Coach Keefer clutched Dud's arm on the sideline.

"Get out there and boot that thing over the bar," the coach said. "I've seen you kick 'em high and far enough! This is the ball game. Make it good!"

Al Dimarzio came to the sideline, massaging his right hand. "Somebody stepped on my hand last play," Dimarzio said. "It's numb. Put somebody in at center, I can't grip the ball!"

Dud looked around, then looked at Coach. Nothing ever happened to rugged Al Dimarzio.

There was no substitute center. Whitey Howell had come to the sideline. He said, "I've snapped the ball some fooling around with Al, Coach. I'll go in at center."

"Okay, okay, get out there! Benton, report in for Dimarzio. Call a time out!" Keefer gave Dud a shove. "The Referee places the ball ready for play and we're diddling around here on the sideline, we'll get a five-yard penalty for delay-of-the-game!"

The teams lined up. Dud marked the spot, as near exactly seven yards behind the line of scrimmage as he could. Eric crouched to take the snapback and place the ball. He called, "Hut! Hut! Hut!"

On the third "Hut!" Whitey Howell snapped the ball. The leather oval sailed far above Dud's head. He stood there, paralyzed. But Eric leaped erect and ran after the ball which was bouncing erratically ten yards behind Dud. Ram linemen had rushed to try to block the kick.

Eric fielded the ball, turned, and dodged a pair of grasping arms. Dud blocked another charging Ram but two more chased after Eric. Other Ram defenders realized there would be no kick and closed off the outside lane where Eric was heading.

Paul Field and tight end Bob Burch, blocking for the place-kick effort, turned when they heard no *thunk* of foot meeting football. They dashed into the end zone, waving arms, yelling at Eric for the ball.

Eric was in the arms of a tackler, actually almost down when he threw the ball. The pass could not have gone straighter. The ball hung like a balloon for Paul Fields to grab.

Touchdown! Six points for the Packers!

Playing time expired on the play. Officials and coaches agreed that a try for point after touchdown was not necessary and called it off. Penalties and incomplete passes had made the game so long that it was now ten minutes past the starting time for the Cowboys-Falcons second game of the evening.

Packers, 6; Rams, 0.

Eric shrugged off whacks on the back and hugs from teammates. Dud said, "Man, you're something else! How do you do it!"

His pal eyed Dud, said, "Remember when I heaved a pass after catching Keefer's punt? You'd been wondering whether I was all that good. Well, when a guy completes a heave like I got off out there—he's not good at all! It's just done with mirrors!"

CHAPTER SIX

Not in the Book

FOUR SMALL STUFF League teams played Friday night games during the regular season schedule. Two teams played a Small Stuff game after the younger Smaller Stuff League games Saturday night.

Saturday morning following the Packer win over the Rams, Dud was waiting for Eric to come out and hold for him to practice place kicks. Eric's grandmother came to the door. She was a white-haired, pleasant-faced lady not quite as tall as her grandson. She smiled at Dud.

"Quote: tell Dud I'll be out in a second. Unquote," she said. "Eric's talking on the phone."

It was more than a second but not very long

before Eric came. "Get your bike," he said. "Dimarzio just finished helping his dad freshen the football field lines. You never told me Mr. Dimarzio was the City Park groundskeeper. Anyway, Al said it was okay to practice kicking at a goal post, if we don't mess up the lines. He wants to practice snapping for the hold. I told him we'd be right over."

They pedaled half a block, then Eric said, "Maybe my old man was right. Maybe he never gave me the snow job I thought."

"Snow job?" Dud looked puzzled.

"Yeah, snow job. My dad could write a book on Football, The Be-All, End-All. He was always giving me the chapter on Mental Attitude, maybe the one on Football Is Like Life, too."

Eric made a little head shake. "You and Dad would hit it off great," he said. "You both think football is THE thing!"

Dud shot a quick look at his friend. Eric was frowning. Dud felt uneasy. "Look," he said. "Sounds as though you and your dad don't exactly see eye-to-eye. You don't have to talk about it to me."

"I guess I want to talk. I've been bothered all week, mostly all I think about is—is—well, you can't know how it is to have had football—*playing* football—rammed down your throat since you can remember!"

Eric drew in a long breath and when he let it out it seemed almost a sigh.

"Dad was All Southwest quarterback when he played in college. He brought Bill and me up on football. He took Bill to games when his hands were more of a size to grip a hotdog than a football, and it was the same with me. I remember Mom really gave it to him because he let me drip mustard all over a snow suit while he whooped and yelled at a game he took me to.

"He was always analyzing the game—at the stadium and afterward, even at the dinner table. You better believe that we went out for teams in organized leagues as soon as we were old enough. Bill went for the whole bit all the way. I don't know whether I really liked football all that much, but I was good at it. And I would force myself to try anything that Bill did!"

They rode a half-block before Eric went on.

"The big reason I'm with Gram while Mom and Dad are away—I could have stayed with my aunt—is because I felt like a big zero for letting Dad down. Well, the other day I got a letter from Dad. He'd heard from Gram about our deal. He congratulated me on 'growing up some' and said he hoped the Packers won the Small Stuff League championship, but whether we won or finished last, he was proud of me."

They came to City Park. While they locked their bikes in the bicycle rack, Eric said thoughtfully, "It made me think more than if he had got sore because I was playing here instead of staying with the team in Texas. So, now I don't know from nothing! We could drop off the team and—and—well, sort of settle things, huh?"

Dud just shook his head. Something about Eric's tone—the lame way he ended his question—made Dud wonder. Did Eric really want to drop out of football?

Al Dimarzio snapped the ball back from the line where the referee would place it after a touchdown. The ball was face high to Eric, who was crouched on one knee seven yards behind Dimarzio. Eric's grab and placement was so smooth that it seemed to be one motion. Dud kicked. The leather oval soared over the crossbar and squarely between the uprights.

"Seventeen good ones out of twenty tries." Dimarzio nodded. "And this guy has only been booting placements a couple of weeks!"

"It should have been twenty for twenty," Dud said. "You and Eric work so well, a fellow should never miss!"

"Even the pro kickers blow one now and then," Eric said.

"Let's try some from farther back," Dud suggested.

He kicked five with Eric placing the ball on the ten yard line. Four were good, one was wide. Eric moved to the twelve. Dud missed two, one wide and one short. From the fifteen he lifted two over the bar, then kicked one wide, and two short.

"Counting the ten yards the posts are behind the goal line, you're booting twenty-five yards," Dimarzio said. "Not too many kids thirteen and under kick a ball that far, place kick or punt."

"Hi, guys." Whitey Howell had come through the gate in the fence around the football field without the boys noticing him. He said, "Happened to be riding by. How about showing me how to make good snapbacks, Al?"

"You sure need someone to show you!" Dimarzio grunted. "That thing you did last night—man!"

Whitey glanced quickly at Dud. "That big Ram guard hit my arm just before the ball left my hand!"

Nobody said anything. Whitey glared at Dud. "I didn't do it on purpose, no matter what you've told them!"

"I haven't told anybody anything."

"Yeah, I bet! How'd you like a fat lip for that big mouth!"

Whitey took a step toward Dud, fists clenched. Dud did not move. Al Dimarzio stepped quickly between them. Big Al shoved Whitey hard enough that he went backward three steps.

"What's the matter with you guys? You're teammates!" Dimarzio eyed Whitey, then Dud. "Save your fight for guys on other teams!"

"Dimarzio is right." Eric half-nudged, half pushed Dud away.

"Okay, that's it," Dimarzio said. "Ride me home on your bike bar, Whitey. I came with Dad on the truck."

After Dimarzio and Howell left, Eric said, "What were you supposed to have told us?"

Dud told his friend how Whitey Howell had accused him of dogging it to make Eric look good, and said he would get even.

"I should have kept Dimarzio from stopping it. Howell ought to be belted around!" Eric shook his head. "I bet you would have taken him apart! But I was thinking like Dimarzio—for the good of the team. Hey, listen to Rogel, will you? How's that for a guy changing his tune?"

CHAPTER SEVEN

Up High

COACH KEEFER talked to the Packers before warmup calisthenics. It was the practice following the Rams game. He carried a clip board with a page of notes.

"I have heard coaches say that anytime they win they are satisfied," he began. "I cannot go along with such philosophy. I am *gratified* that we squeaked past the Rams, but far from *satisfied*. I could never be satisfied when a team I coached turned over the ball five times through errors; failed to score through consistent play; and was saved from being scored upon only by mistakes of the other team."

He consulted the clip board.

"We had three turnovers because our pass protection broke down," he went on. "Rogel was rushed so hard he did not have time to set up to pass, and they intercepted. We have to improve our pass-protection blocking. I am sure Rogel knows that it is better to 'eat the football,' not throw it at all and take the loss. He must remember that fact, and do it! The Rams recovered two of our four fumbles."

The Packer coach stopped a moment and a twinkle came into his eyes.

"The annual award to the best college football player is named after John W. Heisman," Keefer said. "He deserves a place in the list of great coaches. One of the stories told about Heisman is that he once told a squad he coached that a football is an inflated elliptical item used as the ball in a contest between eleven men on a side. And that it was better they should have succumbed as infants than to fumble the ball in a game.

"Now, I would not want any of you fellows to go home and tell your parents I said anything like that to you. But let me impress upon you that the football is something to be cherished when you have it. *Don't get fancy and carry it like you were merely lugging a bag of trash that could be dropped with no problem!*"

"All right," Keefer finished. "We'll hit the dummies after warmup drill. Then we'll block and tackle live—after which we will scrimmage!"

Keefer worked with individual players during the scrimmage. Manny Dillon allowed a ballcarrier to get around him. Keefer whistled the play dead.

"You cornerbacks," the coach said. "If you can't make the tackle when they come at you with a sweep, you do what every cornerback is supposed to do—turn the ballcarrier in. You cannot depend on your safety man. He will probably be blocked. If the ballcarrier gets by you, there is nobody to bar the door!"

After that practice Dud was thankful that his physical condition had improved to where he could take a rugged workout and not collapse. He and Eric rode their bikes homeward with no conversation.

When they pulled into the Benton driveway, Dud said, "He really worked us. But don't you think Coach poured it on more than we deserved? After all, we *did* win!"

Eric regarded him a moment, then made the little head shake that Dud was beginning to expect.

"Is this the same guy who got me to play football because he was dedicated to the Packers and Coach Keefer!" Eric asked with a laugh. "Okay. I told you once that you would learn some football facts of life. One is that any coach worthy of being called a coach keeps after his team to put out the best they can."

Dud watched his friend closely, asked, "It

didn't bug you to have the coach talk like he did about the interceptions?"

Eric said nothing for a moment. When he did speak, Dud wondered whether Eric really answered his question.

"Look," Eric said. "I still feel the way I did when you jobbed me into signing up to play with the Packers. You ought to have played under some coaches I know! Keefer didn't say anything new. I did know I should have eaten the football three or four times. I never claimed I was perfect. You ready to call off this thing we've got tangled in?"

Dud grinned, shook his head. He wondered again what Eric would have done if he had nodded that he would quit, and let Eric out of the bargain.

Eric Rogel took the Bear kickoff and ran it back thirty-six yards. The Packer offense started from very good field position, only four yards short of midfield.

It required only seven plays to get the ball into the end zone. The biggest gain came from a twenty-eight yard pass to Paul Field. The lanky split end grabbed Eric's heave from midfield and drove to the Bear seventeen before he was tackled.

After Klock plunged over from the two for the touchdown, Dud stood with head down, silently mouthing the short-step, long-step-and-kick routine while Eric barked signals. Dud booted the try-for-point over the crossbar.

Packers, 7; Bears, 0.

The scoring drive had used up more than half the first quarter. The kickoff to the Bears was brought back to their fifteen.

A smash into the line netted the Bears a scant three yards. They ran a sweep. The ballcarrier thundered around the Packer right flank. Matt Fernandez, right end of the Packer defense unit, fought off a blocker. The ballcarrier slanted out, trying to turn the corner. Dud did not know that his sudden move toward the sideline evaded a block. He helped Fernandez and right linebacker Boyd Mason smear the play.

They hit the ballcarrier hard. The football squirted from the Bear's arms. Fernandez pounced on the oval and snuggled it into a pocket of thighs, abdomen, hands and arms.

Packer ball on the Bear twenty. Eric Rogel mixed line smashes, sweeps and fake passes. Pete Granger romped through a hole off-tackle when Eric faked a pass and pitched to him the fifth play. A second Packer touchdown. Dud kicked another perfect PAT. Packers, 14; Bears, 0.

"This one'll be easy," Manny Dillon said. "Those guys *have* to lose a lot of drive when they're fourteen points down in the first quarter!"

Manny ought to knock off talk like that, Dud thought. Every time he yaps about a team being easy, they come on like a prairie fire!

The Bears scored midway of the second period. They ran a successful sweep for the point after touchdown and the scoreboard showed Packers, 14; Bears, 7. With three minutes of playing time left in the second quarter, the Packers moved the ball into Bear territory.

"Pros score td's with a lot less time than three minutes," Manny Dillon observed. "Rogel could get us another one before the half. Wouldn't it be nice to have a two-touchdown lead then?"

It would be great, Dud thought. Maybe Eric will find Field or Burch or somebody open for another long pass.

Granger and Klock made just over eight yards in two carries. Third down and short yardage. Would Eric go for the first down or throw? Coach Keefer sent a substitute out from the bench. He clutched Eric's arm as the Packers huddled, and said something to the quarterback. When the ball was snapped, it was clear the "something" had been a play Keefer wanted called.

Eric faded two steps, looking downfield as though searching for an open receiver. A Bear in the secondary yelled, "Pass! Watch it, he's going to throw!"

Linemen and two linebackers charged all-out in a blitz.

Eric abruptly tucked the ball against his body, and drove through a gaping hole left by the rushing defense. The quarterback-draw play worked as well as it had when Keefer introduced it in dummy

scrimmage. Eric slanted past the remaining linebacker. He stiff-armed the cornerback's tackle try,
then faked the safety man "out of his shoes." He
raced on into the end zone.

But officials brought the ball back to the Bear
sixteen. Eric had stepped out of bounds in evading
the safety. Replacements came from the Bear
bench; fresh boys with instructions from their
coach on making defensive adjustment. The Bears
stopped Dick Klock with a scant yard gain the next
play.

Pete Granger was smothered at the thirteen
trying to slant off-tackle. Eric called an option
pass-run, was well defensed by linebackers. He finally threw a safety-valve pass to Whitey Howell out
in the flat zone. Howell caught the ball and was immediately slammed to the ground. No gain.

Fourth down, eight to go for first down, thir-
teen yards to the goal line. Coach Keefer grabbed
Dud's arm. "Get out there," the coach said.
"Loosen your kicking leg before Rogel calls signals.
Boot that thing through there!"

Dud stood behind Eric, crouched for the
placement. The kick would be from the twenty
yard line, five yards farther than he had ever
boosted one over the bar.

"Hut! Hut! Hut!"

The snap. Eric placed the ball. Dud put all the
force he owned into the swing of his leg. The ball
cleared the crossbar by five feet.

Packers, 17; Bears, 7.

The teams trotted off the field for halftime intermission seconds after the kickoff that followed Dud's three-pointer. Dud Benton was up on Cloud Nine.

Coach Keefer passed out praise, and pointed out some things that could be improved. When an official came and advised that intermission time was nearly over, the Packer coach spoke to the squad as a whole.

"You played good football thus far and I'm proud of you. But if there is any thought in your minds that the Bears are beaten—forget it! They are a sound football team. They came back strong after the fumble that set up our second touchdown. They will not fold because they are ten points down now. Depend on it, the Bears will come back real tough!"

The Bears lost no time in showing that Keefer's assessment of them could not have been more correct.

They brought the second-half kickoff back to their thirty-one. They began a steady drive that moved the ball relentlessly toward the Packer end zone. Three first downs. No spectacular long runs or passes, just hard-hitting short yardage gains that ate up time as well as ground.

Barely three minutes of the eight-minute quarter Small Stuff Football League rules provided was left to play when the Bear fullback rammed up the middle into the end zone. They made the point after touchdown.

Packers, 17; Bears, 14.

Then the Bear defense stopped the Packer offense cold. Eric failed to make it on a fourth-and-four option pass-run. It was the Bears' ball as the third quarter ended.

They dominated play throughout the final period. But a penalty halted one drive. A pass intercepted by Dimarzio gave the Packers possession with three minutes and five seconds to play. A series gaining a first down might whittle time down to where they could have killed the clock. But Eric's third down pass was intercepted.

Bears' ball at the midfield mark. Fifty-eight seconds to the end of the game.

"We can hold 'em!" Manny Dillon called to Dud as the defense unit came out.

"We just *have* to hold 'em!"

The Bear quarterback ran a play action pass. A receiver cut across into Dillon's area. The pass was caught. Manny hit the receiver a second's fraction after the catch. Five yard gain. Forty-two seconds left.

It'll be a pass, Dud thought. They may throw it on my side.

The play started like a pass then turned into a sweep when the quarterback flipped the ball backward to his halfback. A guard pulled out of the line and headed the interference. Two backs were ahead of the ballcarrier to block. *If you can't make the tackle, turn the ballcarrier in.* Words Coach had said burned through Dud's thoughts. He did not know whether he could make the tackle. Should he try, or slant out to turn the ballcarrier in?

In the moment of indecision a blocker cut him down. As he crashed to the ground, Dud saw Matt Fernandez lose his battle to fight off a double-team block.

The ballcarrier turned the corner. A blocker washed the legs from beneath Hans Hausse, the safety behind Dud Benton.

Touchdown!

It did not matter that the Bear PAT pass fell incomplete. They kicked off, stopped Eric Rogel's return and the clock ran out of time.

Bears, 20; Packers, 17.

Dud Benton walked slowly off the field. Wouldn't he ever learn? Coach had stressed the very thing he had not done.

He had never felt lower.

CHAPTER EIGHT

The Pack Will Be Back

GRANDMA ROGEL was at the bicycle rack when Dud and Eric came from the football field. She said hello to Dud and turned to Eric: "I only saw the end of the game. I'm sorry you lost."

"I couldn't care less!" Eric shrugged.

"Eric Rogel! That's some way to talk! You simply cannot—"

"Just a sec, Gram!" Eric interrupted hastily. "I didn't mean to sound like I don't care whether we lose! I just meant I couldn't care less if *anybody* saw the game. Losing like we did when we practically had it won!"

"Well, all right." Mrs. Rogel seemed mollified.

She said, "Put your bicycle in the station wagon with Eric's, Dudley. You may as well ride home in the car."

"Thanks, but I'd rather ride my bike." Dud flashed a look at Eric, then added, "I'm the guy who lost the game after we practically had it won!"

"Hey, I didn't say *you* lost the game!"

"Why didn't you? Might as well tell it like it is!"

Dud did not wait for Eric to answer. He threw his leg over the bike saddle and pedaled away from City Park, leaving Eric and his Grandmother looking at each other with surprised faces.

The next morning Dud was sitting on the step outside the back door when Whitey Howell turned his bicycle into the Benton drive. Dud looked up.

"I guess I've gone past seven or eight times," Whitey said.

"I know. Mom saw you and finally asked me if you were somebody I was supposed to meet."

"I've been trying to work up nerve to stop. I wondered if you'd throw me out!"

Dud looked surprised. Whitey moved uncomfortably, eyed Dud a moment, dropped his gaze and said slowly, "It's not easy for a guy to own up that he's been a stinker! I felt bad enough after that center-snap. Then shooting off like I did when you guys were practicing field goals—well, I know how you feel!"

"Uh-uh." Dud shook his head. "You didn't lose a game we had won!"

"I could have. At least, we would have tied the Rams if Rogel hadn't turned that wild snapback into a touchdown pass! You would have made the field goal."

A silence hung between the boys a space of time before Whitey broke it. "Dimarzio ought to have punched me himself," he said. "I haven't felt right since. I started wondering whether I made a horrible snap because I was sore about losing my job to Rogel, even though I knew that Ram guard hit my arm. Anyway, I wanted to tell you not to let things get you down. I—"

Whatever Whitey Howell intended saying was never said. Grandma Rogel's station wagon turned into the drive. Whitey headed his bicycle toward the street. He said, "Tell Rogel I admit he's a better quarterback than I am. No hard feelings. See you at practice."

Eric came from the Rogel garage. He glanced toward Howell, pumping his bike down the street, then looked inquiringly at Dud.

"Came to cheer me up," Dud said. "Figures he knows how I feel because he *could* have made the Ram game a tie. He's nuts!"

Dud drew in a long breath. He had thought things through. He had come to a decision. It would be too bad if Eric went along with the thing about dropping out of football. But whether he did

or not, Dudley Benton was quitting. He would tell
Eric now and hand in his uniform, pads and helmet
to Coach tomorrow.

"Nobody knows how a fellow feels when he finally gets conscious that he's a drag to the team,"
Dud said. "I'm not going to—"

"Hold it!" Eric interrupted. "Don't say something you'll wish you hadn't!" He gave Dud a sharp
look. "Like you are no good to the Packers and
you're gonna quit!"

"How'd you know that is what I'm going to
do?"

"I didn't really know." Eric hesitated, then
said, "Gram read me off pretty good for talking like
I did last night about losing the game. She said I
ought to thank you over and over for getting me to
play football and, quote: put playing the game and
being compared to Bill's achievements in a rational
relationship. Unquote."

Dud stared at his friend. Eric grinned. "Telling
it like it is," he said, "I apologize. You had a right
to think I was handing you a left-handed gripe. But
I wasn't. Remember I blew a fourth-and-one setup?
Remember I threw an interception with less than a
minute to play? I was disgusted with a character
named Rogel. If any one guy lost the ballgame, I'm
the one!"

Still Dud stared. Eric said, "You talk about a
fellow finally getting conscious—then get conscious! Now, I kept urging Gram to hurry so we'd

make it home in time to watch the game on TV. It's the Green Bay Packers and the Los Angeles Rams today. Come on, we'll watch the big guys batter each other!"

Dud kept mulling things over while the television announcer talked about the professional Rams and Packers. He had wondered whether Eric would quit the Packers even when Eric asked why he didn't get smart, and give up on football. Now he wondered more than ever.

Not long ago an assignment for English class at school had been to look up definitions of a dozen words. One of the list was rational. Among the dictionary meanings for rational was 'showing reason, not foolish or silly; sensible.' Eric must have given his grandmother some reason to think he had put playing football in sensible relationship.

". . . return to the glory days of Coach Vince Lombardi's Packers of the 1960's. The Pack was not only the pride of Green Bay fans. They were recognized everywhere as one of the GREAT football teams. . . ."

It was wonderful that Eric finally saw he would be lost without football. It was great for him and for the Small Stuff League Packers.

". . . this comparatively small city of Green Bay," the television voice said, "supports their beloved Packers with loyalty rarely equaled—never surpassed—by fans of big city professional teams. Even after defeats in the dark years that followed the Lombardi era, the rallying cry in Wisconsin was The Pack Will Be Back! . . ."

The smooth voice of the announcer managed to bring in praise for Green Bay Packer fans several more times. He kept mentioning loyalty to the Packers, and The Pack Will Be Back slogan.

Dud sighed. It wasn't that he was not loyal to the Small Stuff Packers. Turning in his equipment and dropping off the squad would be showing a kind of loyalty. Coach would not have to put him in games if he wasn't there.

The Small Stuff Football League Pack would be back. One loss did not put them all that far back! But it would be easier when they did not have to contend with a Dud!

CHAPTER NINE

A Different Slant

AL DIMARZIO trotted to the sideline after meeting with the Falcon captains and officials. "Won the toss," he reported. "We receive at the south end of the field."

"Good." Coach Keefer inclined his head, then swept his gaze over the Packers gathered around him. "I thought we were better than the Falcons in the Jamboree," he said. "I still think we are the better team. We can take them if we play as we are capable of playing. Rogel and I have gone over the offensive game plan we are going to follow.

"I have never believed so-called pep talks can take the place of coaching and solid work, and we do that in practice time. What I am about to say is not meant as a pep talk. However, since the loss to the Bears, there has been some loose talk about one player losing the game."

He waited a brief space of time, then went on.

"Every play in a football game *could* result in the winning touchdown being scored, or prevented. A missed blocking assignment, a missed tackle, a ballcarrier dodging the wrong way and being tackled—there are so many opportunities to make or miss plays that may count big in the final result. No one player—or two, or three or what have you—can be blamed for losing or given credit for winning all alone. Keep in mind that a football game is a contest between *teams*, not individuals.

"All right, get out there and play team football!"

They ran to positions to receive the kickoff.

Eric Rogel took a short kick in front of the fifteen yard line. He sized up Falcon coverage, ran five steps straight up the field, then veered to the right. But what had been a clear lane was suddenly closed by the Falcon who had booted the kickoff. He forced Eric out of bounds six yards short of the midfield stripe. Good field position for the Packers.

In the huddle, Eric said, "Keefer wants to establish a running game before we try any open stuff. Granger inside left tackle. You guys up front block and give him some daylight to shoot at!"

Pete Granger took Eric's pitchout and slanted

left. Tackle Doug Flinn blocked his man out; guard Fred Skinner blocked his man in. Granger cut through the good hole as Al Dimarzio mowed down the middle linebacker.

The play went for a nine yard gain. Eric said, "Way to carry the mail, Pete! And you guys blocked! We'll hit 'em with the same, only Dick carries. Hut!"

Dick Klock fell in behind Granger as Eric feinted right, pivoted and floated the ball to the running back. Flinn and Skinner again did a job on their assignments. Dimarzio drew a bead on the linebacker. Granger went upfield keeping his bulk between Klock and the cornerback. The safety man came up and made a good tackle. But the ball was on the Falcon thirty-two when the referee blew it dead.

"First and ten!" the official called.

Falcon defenders dug in. It took three smashes into the line to gain another first down at the Falcon seventeen. Klock was stopped for a scant two yard gain. Granger made only three smashing over guard. Eric faked a pitchout and drifted wide on a quarterback keeper. For a moment it seemed as though the Falcon defense was completely fooled. But one defensive back was alert, spotted the ball carried behind Eric's hip. He spilled the Packer quarterback at the nine yard line.

Fourth down and two yards to make for a first down. Eric looked pleadingly toward the bench.

But Coach Keefer had Dud Benton already moving onto the field.

Eric crouched at the sixteen. Dud stood ready, his thoughts a kaleidoscopic riot. *I can't keep you from turning in your equipment. But I can tell you that you are one hundred percent wrong in thinking such action would help the Packers!* That was what Coach Keefer had said when Dud talked with him before the first practice after the Bear game.

Okay, so you were mowed down and a ballcarrier went all the way! You think you're the first defensive back ever got outsmarted? You're nutty to let a thing like that get you down.

Oddly, Dud thought that Eric's reaction had nothing about his being freed, if Dud quit.

You're going to make up for those six points you think you cost us. Coach sure hadn't sounded like he was just talking. *Benton, you've worked hard and developed into an asset as a kicker.*

Dimarzio snapped the ball perfectly. Eric set it perfectly. Dud Benton booted the ball squarely between the uprights.

Packers, 3; Falcons, 0.

Dud felt warm and good. As he trotted off the field, he caught sight of Eric who flashed him one of the biggest smiles he had ever seen. He was very, very happy that Coach and Eric had persuaded him not to quit the squad.

The Falcons took the kickoff following the Packer field goal, ran the ball back to their thirty-seven. Then the pattern of their offense game plan was set on the first play from scrimmage.

A back sifted through running a short pass route. The split end, tight end and flankerback ran deeper pass patterns. Dud tried frantically to pick the right man as a wide receiver and another back came into his area. He chose the wrong man.

The wide receiver made a fine catch and raced down the sideline to the Packer forty before he was shoved out of bounds.

Another short pass complete. Second down and four. A slash off-tackle for barely two yards. Then another pass—a "bomb" thrown sixteen yards in the air into the grasp of the split end two yards behind Dud Benton. Touchdown!

Trying a kick for the point after touchdown, the Falcon kicker lifted the ball no more than six feet off the ground. But the scoreboard showed Falcons, 6; Packers, 3.

Twenty-seven seconds to the end of the quarter showed on the clock when the Falcon kickoff carried over the end zone back line. Eric sneaked for six yards from the twenty. Dick Klock plunged through the middle of the line for a first down at the thirty-one as the period ended.

Eric began the second quarter alternating Klock and Granger smashing inside and off the tackles. When the defense tightened, he ran Whitey Howell on a sweep. He came right back with Whitey on a deep reverse. Then Eric kept on a quarterback draw. He faked a pass and again ran the ball from a play-action option. First down at the Falcon twelve.

Trap play up the middle. Good blocking. Handoff. Pete Granger high-kneed through and into the end zone without a Falcon touching him.

Dud came off the bench, kept his head down while he followed the routine of a-small-step-with-the-right-foot-a-big-step-with-the-left-foot-then-kick. The ball rose nicely and soared over the crossbar three feet inside the left upright.

Packers, 10; Falcons, 6.

The Falcons received, carried the kickoff thirty-six yards from the eight, then started attacking again with passes. Short one over the line of scrimmage to the tight end for eight yards. A safety-valve flip to a back in the flat zone when receivers downfield were covered. A fine broken-field run to the Packer eighteen.

Two passes were incomplete, one knocked down and the other underthrown. A smash into the line off a draw-play did not fool Al Dimarzio. He stopped the ballcarrier for no gain. Fourth down and ten. It looked as though the Packers had held.

The scoring play was beautiful.

The Falcon quarterback pitched back to a halfback and a guard pulled out of the line to head interference for what had all the earmarks of a sweep. The Packer defense moved right to smother the play. Then the boy with the ball abruptly stopped, turned and started in the opposite direction as though running a reverse. He handed the ball to the quarterback.

By this time two Falcon receivers were in opposite corners of the end zone. A Packer safety covered one, but the other was completely open. He took the quarterback's pass. Touchdown.

The Falcons tried a sweep for the point after touchdown. The ballcarrier was smothered a yard short of the goal line. No point. Scoreboard figures changed to Falcons, 12; Packers, 10.

Eric Rogel wriggled free of a tackler and ran the kickoff from the six to the twenty-four. Then he began racing the clock. Smashes off tackle and inside tackle. Draw plays when he faked passes and had the defense rushing. One short pass completed to "keep them honest."

Klock smashed through for eight. Granger cracked off tackle for six. A sweep gained twelve. Six seconds showed on the clock before the end of the half. When Eric faded back, defenders raced to cover eligible receivers, yelling, "Pass! Watch it, he's going to throw!"

Paul Field raced around behind Eric and took the ball off his drawn-back-for-a-pass hand. The old Statue of Liberty play never worked better. The Falcon defense was caught committed to stopping a pass. Field had no difficulty beating a safety's forlorn chase to the corner of the field. Packer touchdown!

Dud Benton stood just far enough behind the

spot, waited for the snap and Eric's smooth set—
and added the PAT as though it was practically au-
tomatic.

Packers, 17; Falcons, 12.

Scoreboard figures had not changed when the
gun ending the first half sounded after the Packer
kickoff.

"I have no criticism," Coach Keefer told his
team, after an official notified him that halftime intermission was at the return-to-the-field point. "By
that I don't mean to take away from the Falcons.
They have completed a fantastic percentage of
passes. Perhaps our running game success is
equally fantastic. We are making some changes in
our defensive secondary, and will continue to make
adjustments. Stay in there and battle. I still believe
we are the better team!"

Falcons had the choice to start the second
half. They elected to receive, of course. Dud got off
a fine, high kick. But the Falcons were not bothered by the fact that they started from their eighteen yard line.

Coach Keefer replaced Dud at cornerback with
Whitey Howell. Another replacement was made at
weak safety. No matter. Falcon passes were
grabbed when receivers were covered, when they
were overthrown, when they were underthrown. It
seemed they could do no wrong.

They moved steadily, had a first down at the

Packer eight. Then a fumble apparently halted the drive. But although Al Dimarzio recovered the fumble, an official had spotted a Packer holding. The penalty gave the Falcons first down.

Two passes were incomplete. Then the Packer defense was caught bunching to stop an expected third-down smash. The short, basketball-type toss to an end slanting behind the line of scrimmage scored the touchdown.

Again the try for point failed. Falcons, 18; Packers, 17.

Eric engineered another Packer drive. A hard tackle jarred the ball from Whitey Howell's grasp at the Falcon twelve. A Falcon recovered the fumble. Whitey Howell was almost in tears on the bench.

"We lose this game, it's my fault!" he wailed. "I thought I was squeezing the ball! I lost the game!"

"Knock it off!" Eric growled. "We haven't lost. We can run all night on these guys!"

"Yeah," somebody down the bench said. "And it looks like they can pass all night on us!"

The looks-like-they-can-pass-all-night-on-us seemed to be a dire prophecy. Only four plays were needed to produce another Falcon touchdown. Three of the four were completed passes. The line buck for the point after try failed again. It seemed a no-matter thing. Falcons, 24; Packers, 17.

Pete Granger returned the kickoff to eight

yards short of midfield. Eric Rogel rallied the Packers in the huddle.

"We go from here into the end zone," Eric said confidently, "without giving up possession! Okay! Pete takes it off tackle. Then we line up without a huddle and Dick rams that thing down their throats through the other side. Hut!"

Pete Granger crashed through and ripped into the secondary. He broke a linebacker's tackle-try and ran the ball to the Falcon thirty. The quick play without a huddle caught the Falcons completely by surprise. Dick Klock was only a step away from the goal line when he was knocked out of bounds.

Eric faked a handoff to Granger, then fed the ball to the second back driving through—Klock. He was a yard into the end zone before he was tackled.

Dud Benton added the extra point. Packers, 24; Falcons, 24.

The tie lasted until midway of the final period. Then a receiver sneaked in behind the Packer safety, took a long pass on the five, and trotted into the end zone.

On the bench, Dud Benton thought, they'll try to pass for the point this time, for sure. They don't have a kicker and they haven't made one running yet.

The Falcons did try a pass. Al Dimarzio, smart and uncannily able at reading offensive sets, crashed through and swarmed the passer under before he could pick out a receiver. But scoreboard figures told a sad tale for the Packers—Falcons, 30; Packers, 24.

Two minutes and five seconds registered on the scoreboard clock when Eric faced the Packer offense unit after the kickoff was returned to their thirty-nine.

"We're going to grind it out," Eric said. "You guys carrying that thing, treat it like it was made of glass that would break if you fumbled! Everybody block. We're going to score and beat these guys!"

Grind it out was what they did.

The Falcons threw up an eight man line. Then they brought linebackers up so close that it amounted to a nine-man line, with only two secondary defenders. Eric faked passes but kept the ground attack going relentlessly. Three, four, six— once eight yards on a keeper—got the first downs. Running plays also used up playing time. Less than a minute of playing time remained when the Packers made a first down on the eleven yard stripe.

Klock smashed for two. Timeout to stop the clock. Granger slammed over guard for four. Timeout. Granger right back to crash just inches short of the goal line. Timeout. Four seconds left on the clock.

"This is it," Eric said tensely. "They'll gang up to stop a line smash. Drag a little, Whitey, then dig for the corner of the end zone. I'll hang the ball out there. Grab it!"

The lines banged together. Whitey dragged. It

was doubtful whether Granger, Klock or Eric could have penetrated the defense. But Eric floated a soft pass into the end zone corner and Whitey Howell clutched the ball tightly.

Touchdown. Packers, 30; Falcons, 30.

Dud Benton came from the bench. The clock showed that playing time expired during the touchdown play. This kick would decide whether the Falcons and Packers tied—or the Packers won.

Eric glanced at Dud, opened his mouth to say something then closed it. He pointed to the spot he had picked to set the ball, looked questioningly at Dud. Dud nodded.

Dimarzio's snap came back crisply and true. Eric's smooth motion to place the ball was continuous to his taking the snap. Dud kept his head down, swung his foot and followed through. Exultant yells from his teammates told him the kick was good.

Packers, 31; Falcons, 30.

Then was when the tension hit Dud. He shook like a leaf in a fall breeze. He saw Eric grin, heard his friend say, "You must have ice water instead of blood to take it so cool!"

Then it really hit Dud that he had kicked the winning point. Eric grabbed him around the shoulders. "Five td's they made to our four!" Eric marveled. "But your kicking added up to a win! You ought to have a different slant on things now—for sure!"

CHAPTER TEN

Ride Those Cowboys!

COACH KEEFER was not at the practice field when Al Dimarzio took charge. Al said, "Coach expected to be delayed. He told me to get the dummies out and do the warmup stuff. So, let's go!"

Keefer had still not shown up when Dimarzio's count for the final exercise ended. A volley of comments and questions came from the boys.

"That all you're going to give us? . . . You must be tired, or something! . . . What do we do now 'til Coach comes? . . . What gives with him being late?"

Al Dimarzio surveyed his teammates, shook his head, then said, "Coach warned me you characters would probably still be high from sneaking past the Falcons! He's at a meeting of coaches and Small Stuff League officials. They have to set up things in case there is a tie for the First Half title.

"Pass the ball around. Kick it. The dummies are set up, practice hitting them. Or practice live blocking and tackling each other. Coach'll be here soon."

Eric Rogel looked questioningly at Dud. "What's this First Half business?" Eric asked.

"After each team has played every other team in the league," Dud explained, "the team with the best percentage-wise record of wins and losses is First Half champion. Ties don't count. Everybody starts fresh for the Second Half. That way a team that maybe had rough going but developed has a chance at the Second Half title. At the end of the regular schedule, First Half champs play Second Half champs for the Small Stuff League championship."

"Suppose the team that won the First Half wins the Second Half?"

"Everybody connected with the Small Stuff Football League has asked that question, I think." Dud nodded. "So far it has never happened. If and when it does, the double-champion will play a team of All Stars from other teams in the league."

Eric inclined his head, said, "Logical. Want to practice booting field goals? I'll get Dimarzio to snap for us."

Dud hesitated, eyed his friend. "I know you

won't take this the wrong way," Dud said. "I'm satisfied with my kicking more than some other things.
I'd better hit the dummy. Someday I'm going to be
able to *tackle*—and *block*—I hope!"

Dud was charging the dummy, throwing
blocks and tackles alternately, when Coach Keefer
arrived. The coach came past just as Dud smashed
the stuffed demon clean and hard. "A block like
that might spring a ballcarrier loose for a touchdown," Keefer said. He whistled the boys to gather
before him.

"A three-way tie is possible for the First Half,"
he began. "As of now, the Colts have a two-won,
no-loss, one-tie record. We have two wins and one
loss. The Bears have won one, lost one, and tied a
game. It could happen that the three teams would
end First Half play with identical three wins, one
loss, and one tie records. We made plans today for
a playoff in such event."

The coach stopped a moment, then went on.

"The Rams *could* beat the Colts Saturday,
but I don't think they will. The Colts will probably
win and bring a three-oh-one record into their
game with us next week. So, our job is to take the
Cowboys and make the Colt-Packer game definite
for the First Half championship."

Keefer waited for the boys' excited comments
to stop. Then he said, "Our first job is to get ready
for the Cowboys. I hope none of you feel that their
loss to the Rams by two touchdowns makes us fa-

vorites. Four first string Cowboys were sick that night!

"We have had the weekend to chew over our very fine win and it has been great chewing. I am sure we won't meet a more potent passing game. I am also sure that the Cowboy coach and most of their players noted that the Falcons all but killed us with passes. So, today we start trying to shore up our pass defense!"

Coach Keefer played Whitey Howell, Eric Rogel, Kip Ryskowski and even Dick Klock at secondary defense positions. As he wound up the practice session, Keefer told the squad there would be more of the same in the two remaining practices before the Cowboy game.

Dud Benton had not been used at defense. He wondered if he had been completely cut off from the cornerback job he had held.

Whitey Howell was fussing with the driving chain of his bike when Eric and Dud approached the bicycle rack. He was plainly stalling. Whitey flicked a glance at Dud, then at Eric. He moved nervously, finally eyed Eric.

"I better get this out before I turn chicken and don't say it," Whitey nodded. "My dad was a quarterback for his high school football team. You ever wonder why dads count so much on their kid following in their footsteps?"

"Good question." Eric shrugged. "I know what you mean."

"Dad sputtered plenty when Keefer started

you at my old spot," Whitey went on. "But after watching you run our offense the other night, he said it was a good thing that Coach recognized talent! Didn't make me feel what you could say real great, but Dad was right. I never could have engineered that last quarter drive! You guys sure took me off the hook after my fumble gave them the game!"

Dud and Eric joined in talking Whitey out of any off-the-hook feeling. Dud ended by pounding his chest and letting out a screeching yell.

"Super-hero," he said. "This week I'm the guy who won the game! But remember last week. I was super-goat, the guy who lost the game! Like Coach said, nobody wins a game by himself. And nobody loses a game by himself! You weren't on any bigger hook than I was last week—not as much!"

Whitey Howell eyed Dud, shifted his gaze to Eric and back to Dud.

"You guys could hate me," Whitey said. "I'm glad you both like football so much that you're not that kind!"

After Whitey rode away Dud looked at Eric and grinned. "You guys like football so much," he mused. "I've been wondering. How about that?"

Eric flicked a quick look at his friend, dropped his eyes. "You hinting that you don't like football all that much?" he asked innocently.

"Different slant." Dud nodded. "That's what you told me I should have. Well, how about you?"

Eric grinned, turned away while he snapped

the lock around the spring of his bike saddle. "Skip it," he said.

Cowboys and Packers would clash physically Friday night. But "talk" clashes took place whenever members of the teams met that week.

"They're really confident," Al Dimarzio said after the second Packer practice. "I took some stuff Dad wanted from home yesterday and got to the Park just when the Cowboys were leaving. They socked it to me good! I'm sure glad Coach is hammering us for pass defense. They got real cocky putting out stuff about stopping us cold then passing us dizzy!"

"We'll probably get the needle tomorrow, Eric," Dud said. "Guys from their school have been at the library every time our class has been there. Thursday must be their regular library day, too."

Dud's prediction proved one hundred percent correct. Six boys were in the reference room when Dud, Eric and Pete Granger came into that department of City Library.

Dud recognized a tall boy with dark reddish hair—captain and quarterback of the Cowboy offense unit, safety-man in their six-two-two-one defense. Another boy nudged the tall Cowboy star and whispered loud enough for Dud to hear. "There's the guy who kicked the field goals and points-after, Brick. The other two are the Packer quarterback and their linebuster!"

The boy called Brick turned and surveyed the Packer trio. He grinned. "If you guys are looking for some gimmick," he said, "you're out of luck. We've hidden all the stuff on football."

Eric glanced at the redhead. "You play with some team?" Eric asked.

Brick flushed, then abruptly widened his grin. But a glint was in his eyes. "Naw!" He shrugged. "We're just trying to gather dope on the GREAT quarterbacks. You happen to know any from, say— Texas?"

Eric jerked a quick look at the redhead. Dud was sure that the jibe got to Eric. This was all crazy, anyhow. Eric saw the look Dud gave him. He said in an undertone, "This is old stuff. Get the other guy's goat, our coach used to say."

Dud was surprised to hear Pete Granger speak in an exaggerated drawl. "You 'uns know where to find stuff about Ride the Cowboys? We have to write a paper for English. I reckon a paper about sayings and slogans of the Old West would be something different."

"You mean Ride *'em*, Cowboys! Yeah, we know all about that! That was a yell cowboys used when they were breaking wild horses. Then cowboys used it when they rode steers headed for the slaughter house—*packers*, you could say! They—"

"Sh-h-h! Knock it off!"

One of the Cowboys hissed the warning. A teacher came through the arch separating the reference room from the main part of City Library. She was indisputably a teacher, but not Dud's, Eric's and Pete's teacher.

"John, you disappoint me!" The teacher removed her glasses and pointed them at the boy next to the tall redhead. "You know better! Ride 'em is a contraction of ride *them*. An example of poor usage that we have discussed in class. The phrase should be ride *those* cowboys!

"And nothing of this sort is in your assignment, I might add!"

Almost from the opening kickoff knowledgeable football fans recognized that tonight the Packers were playing much better ball than the Cowboys. Somebody in the stands behind the Packer bench summed things up midway of the first period.

"The Cowboys got some wrong ideas watching the Packers last week. Looks like they convinced themselves all they had to do was stack their defense to turn back the Packer ground game, and riddle them with passes. But it just doesn't figure that a smart coach like Keefer would allow any team to catch his boys short two weeks in a row! And that quarterback! He could play high school ball right now!"

Eric Rogel kept the Cowboy defense off-balance from the first play from scrimmage. He passed when they were set for line smashes. He rolled out and ran the ball himself. He pitched off to Klock, Granger or Howell when they rushed to upset his passing and ball-handling. He marched the Packers methodically up and down the field for three touchdowns the first half.

Dud booted the PAT's almost as though he was a computer-directed machine.

The Cowboys tried passes. But the Packer coverage smothered receivers; the Packer front four defensemen—Coppock, Fisher, Wyatt and Fernandez—harassed and hurried the Cowboy passer.

Keefer was not a close-the-gates-of-mercy coach. With a twenty-one point lead, the Packer coach sent in reserves to play most of the second half. Only once did the Packers threaten to score.

The end result was the lone Cowboy score.

Fourth down at the five-yard line. Coach Keefer called to Dud: "You need the practice more than we need another td. Get out there and kick a field goal."

Dimarzio's snap was not the perfect effort he had always made before. Eric may have been flustered in hurriedly placing the ball; it was not a smooth set. Definitely, Dud's kicking rhythm was ruined.

The kick did not rise. It was blocked by an on-rushing Cowboy lineman. The ball ricocheted from his hands and bounded fifteen yards behind Dud. Another Cowboy, following the blocker, got a lucky bounce, grabbed the ball and took off. He took off all the way into the Packer end zone.

A missed conversion try left scoreboard figures showing Packers, 21; Cowboys, 6. They were unchanged at the final gun.

Pete Granger craned his neck as the Packers left the field. Suddenly he said, "Hey! There they are! Come on, you guys. I've been counting on a chance to get even!"

Dud and Eric followed the husky fullback. Two boys in Cowboy uniforms walked with heads down from the field. The tall one carried his helmet and exposed a shock of brick-red hair.

Pete sidled near the pair of Cowboys, said loudly as though not speaking to anybody in particular, "It sure is a contraction of ride *them* when you're dealing with bound-for-the-Packer-slaughterhouse-characters. You have to remember to make it Ride *those* Cowboys—and did we ever!"

Dud liked the way the redhead lifted his eyes, grinned sheepishly and shook his head. "We had that coming," he said. "Good luck when you try riding the Colts next week!"

CHAPTER ELEVEN

Coach Keefer Plays a Hunch

AL DIMARZIO phoned Dud Saturday morning. Al said, "It's okay if we use the end of the field Dad isn't working on. How about you and Rogel meeting me at City Park?"

"Swell. Eric and I were going to practice kicking over the wire. It'll be better to have a snapperback and a regular goal post to aim at."

Riding their bikes to City Park, Dud and Eric talked about the upcoming Packer-Colt battle.

"They'll be plenty tough to beat," Eric observed. "They're a sound outfit. They move the ball really good."

"Yeah. They've got a kicker, too. He hasn't missed an extra point yet and he's booted five field goals in four games. One of them from the twenty-four—that's a thirty-four yard kick!"

"Good distance for a Small Stuff type kicker," Eric agreed. "But I'd bet you could do better."

"Come off of it! Putting me on will get you nothing!"

"I'm not putting you on. You just don't realize the power you've got. And I don't mean just for a short-legged guy."

"Coach keeps drumming it into me that kicking is more a matter of timing than anything else," Dud said.

They came to City Park. Dud was not especially surprised to see Whitey Howell with Al Dimarzio. Whitey was a basketball nut. You could find him most anytime there was no school, shooting baskets or getting up a scrub game at one of the City Park basketball courts. But the gloomy expressions of Dimarzio and Whitey *were* surprising.

"What's with you guys?" Eric asked. "You look like it's final exam day at school, or something."

"There sure ain't nothing to cheer about." Dimarzio shook his head. "Tell 'em, Whitey."

"It's one of those crazy things you never think would happen," Whitey said. "Pete Granger and I live in the same block. When an ambulance zoomed into our street about an hour ago, siren going full blast, everybody in the block came out. It turned into the Granger drive and pretty quick they brought Pete out on a stretcher.

"Pete and his mom were going to refinish a big

old table. He was helping her move it to the garage. She stumbled on the step down, the table slipped from her hands, knocked Pete to the floor and landed on him. His right ankle is probably broken."

Whitey shook his head, then went on.

"Talk about a bad break—and I don't mean just for Pete! We'll miss his ballcarrying for sure—and what about when we need a punt? Pete's the only guy could get off a decent kick more'n once out of three or four times!"

Dimarzio said, "Looks like somebody ought to be practicing punting real hard."

Eric was eyeing Dud. Dud could practically read his friend's mind.

"Not me!" Dud shook his head. "I watched Coach working with Pete—I couldn't punt!"

"You couldn't boot field goals and points after, either," Eric said. "Didn't you tell me coming out here that kicking is chiefly a matter of timing? You have swell timing booting placekicks."

"Hey!" Al Dimarzio brightened. "We'll practice punting instead of placekicks! I'll center. Dud, you kick to Rogel and Whitey. It'll give them practice catching and running kicks back, too."

The Packers received the news about Pete Granger at the first practice to prepare for the Colts. "X-rays indicate no fracture," Keefer told them, "and there are no internal injuries. His ankle is badly bruised and some ligaments are badly torn.

Pete will be wearing a cast for several weeks. He will play no more football this season."

Coach Keefer surveyed the group.

"Any of you think you can learn in four days to punt passably?" he asked. "I'll pass on all the knowledge of kicking I have."

Nobody said anything. Dud squirmed under quick glances from Eric and Dimarzio. What if he had got off a couple of fairly decent punts at City Park? That didn't make a fellow a punter. And Pete Granger had been more than just a punter. Whoever replaced Pete needed to be a blocker, able to carry the ball, too.

Whitey Howell finally broke the silence. Whitey told Keefer of the kicking practice at City Park. "Rogel and I had a try at punting," he finished. "Benton kicked a lot better than either of us. He kicked some real good ones. Dud can do the job, if we need a punt!"

Keefer looked sharply at Dud, inclined his head. Something about the coach's expression made Dud wonder if his nod meant something— like maybe he had been thinking of Dud Benton?

Dud's leg and foot felt as if it weighed more than a hundred pounds. He and Eric and Whitey and Klock and Dimarzio had been asked to stay after the coach dismissed the squad. Dimarzio snapped. The three backfield starters chased the punts.

The first three were horrible. Dud would gladly have called it a day. But Keefer said, "Your form is basically good. No one expects you to start right off booting forty yard kicks. Two things: keep your eye on the ball from the drop to contact with your foot; follow through all the way after contact is made."

Some of his kicks slid off the side of Dud's foot. He hit the ball a few times so high up that the force came more from his shin than foot. "Shanked it," Keefer said the first time that happened. "You took your eye off the ball before your foot met it."

Some of the punts were not too terribly poor.

Dud quit counting after he had kicked fifty-three. He was sure that he kicked at least twice that many more before Keefer called, "That's all. Seventy efforts, Benton—and forty-two were better than fair punts."

His eyes twinkled then and Coach added, "If you dream of punting, remember: keeping your eye on the ball, proper timing and follow-through make a punter."

After warmup exercises at the next practice, Coach Keefer talked to his offense unit.

"I told you fellows at our first workout that I would try not to expect too much of you and not over-coach," he said. "We have run our plays from a basic T-formation. You have done a grand job with the few pass-action runs and option variations

I stuck in. Granger and Klock have gained a lot of yardage on power smashes. Howell runs sweeps and reverses well. Now, we are forced to re-arrange our offensive backfield."

The coach stopped speaking for what seemed to Dud a long space of time. Dud thought the coach would say that Benton would go in when a punt—or field goal try—was the play. He wondered briefly who would start in Pete Granger's place.

"Howell will shift to left half and Benton will be at right half." When Keefer did speak, his tone was confident. "Admittedly, I am playing a hunch. Benton has developed into a fine blocker and he will mostly block in our new alignment. My hunch is that having him in the game if and when a punting situation comes, will take away the edge the Colts would have if we had to advertise a kick by sending Benton in from the bench."

Dud's pulse quickened. He was aware that Dimarzio and Eric and Howell and Klock looked at him, and that none of them registered doubt. And, abruptly, he began to feel different.

Coach had noted his extra work at the blocking dummy and had complimented him. Coach had also complimented his kicking. After six weeks of hard, rough work, Dudley Benton was not the easy-going waterboy of last year.

He was not all trembly and mushy inside. Just maybe Dudley Benton was no longer a dud.

CHAPTER TWELVE

Colts Versus Packers

AL DIMARZIO won the toss and elected to receive. Butterflies fluttered in Dud Benton's suddenly empty abdomen when he took his place for the kickoff. Migosh, what if the kick came to him?

The kickoff sailed end-over-end straight down the middle. Colt tacklers raced downfield. Eric caught the ball in full stride.

He faked the first tackler then darted right. He slanted back past a second tackler who dove vainly where Eric had been. But the Colt coverage was good. Eric was smothered under tacklers at the Packer thirty-one.

"Coach knows the Colts have scouted us," Eric said in the huddle. "So far we haven't thrown a bomb on our first play from scrimmage. He wants one now. Field runs a deep down-and-out pattern to the left. Howell goes a little shorter route to the right, but down there a ways. I'll hang that thing out there for whichever one gets open. You guys blocking, hold their rushers off long enough for the receivers to get down there—and me to heave it! Hut!'"

Coach Keefer's strategy caught the Colt secondary defense off-balance. They did not react immediately. Field and Howell had defensive backs beaten, but the safety man was tearing over to help cover Paul Field. Eric wisely chose not to throw to the split end.

Eric's pass to Whitey Howell would have been difficult to improve on. The ball led the receiver just right. Whitey reached out, pulled the ball in and tucked it in firm grasp between his hand and chest. The Packer halfback was two yards behind the defensive back when he caught the pass; he was more than three yards ahead of the Colt when he crossed the goal line.

Eric crouched at the ten; Dud stood relaxed and waiting. Al Dimarzio snapped the ball and Eric set it smoothly. Dud took his step-and-kick, kept his head down, swung his leg in the follow-through. Then he heard the concerted groan from teammates on the sideline, looked up and saw the official down under the goal posts swinging his arms to indicate the kick was wide, no good.

Dud stood on the sideline beside Eric while the Packers lined up for the kickoff to the Colts. "How did it happen?" Dud's tone held bewilderment. "I didn't do anything different!"

"My hold was maybe a little off. Maybe you hit the ball a little off-center." Eric shrugged. "Even the pro specialists blow a kick now and then. Forget it. You'll make the next one."

"Yeah." Agreement came from Manny Dillon. He stood the other side of Eric. Coach Keefer did not consider Dillon as fast getting down under a kickoff as another boy. "That little old point won't matter," Manny said. "You guys on offense will put oodles of points on the scoreboard tonight—and our defense will kill the Colts!"

"Don't say a thing like that!" Dud threw his hands to the sides of his head in pretended horror. "Every time you brag, things happen to us!"

Afterward, Dud wondered. It was superstitious—silly—to think that Manny Dillon had anything to do with giving the other team a boost. Still, the Colts ran the ball for a first down after the kickoff. Then they mixed short passes, line smashes, sweeps and line bucks for three straight first downs.

Coach Keefer sent replacements from the bench, with instructions for defensive adjustments. The Colt coach countered by sending a substitute into the Colt backfield, no doubt with a play.

Keefer lost the coaching strategy contest—

perhaps more correctly, the Colt offense defeated the Packer defense.

Colts' ball at the Packer twelve, first down. The Colts abandoned their buck, sweep, pass, buck pattern. They came from the huddle into a spread formation. The Packer defense tried to adjust, but a Colt receiver sneaked behind Manny Dillon when the Packer cornerback covered a decoy receiver running a short route. The pass was "right on the money." Nothing but atmosphere was in front of the receiver. He raced into the end zone for the tying touchdown.

Their kicker split the uprights for the PAT. Figures on the scoreboard changed to Colts, 7; Packers, 6. Seven seconds more than half the eight-minute playing time allowed for Small Stuff League quarters showed on the clock.

Packer offensive team members settled headgears to go out for the Colt kickoff. Eric said, "Looks like this could turn into another donnybrook like we had with the Falcons! That means a swinging, everybody-scores setup. We'd better get some points on the board every time we have the ball!"

But what was supposed to be a free-scoring game settled into a slogging, hard-hitting defensive battle.

The Packers managed one first down. Then three plays left the ball at the thirty-eight, four yards to make for first down. Punt formation. Dud

stood in the deep position. Good snapback. Dud
got off a punt that angled out of bounds at the Colt
forty-two. Out-of-bounds punts cannot be run back.
Twenty yards from the line of scrimmage.

Not a record punt, Dud thought. But counting
the thirteen yards I was behind the line of scrimmage, I booted the ball thirty-three yards. Not bad
for me!

The Colts marked up a first down, connected
on a short pass for eight yards the first play of the
next series. A line buck netted no gain. A third-
down pass was incomplete. They punted from their
forty-one.

It was a high, spiraling kick that Dick Klock
misjudged badly after signaling a fair catch. The
ball sailed over his head. It took a Colt roll and was
not blown dead until it stopped on the Packer
twenty-seven.

That play ended the first quarter. The Packers
had lost five yards on the punt exchange. They took
possession of the ball to start the second period.

Domination of play by the defensive units continued. Three plays gained but six yards. Dud
punted. Colt offensive efforts ran into a tough
Packer defense. A Colt punt. They gained seven
yards on the exchange.

Play became a bang-batter-pass struggle between the thirty yard lines. On their third posses-

sion, a busted play in the Packer backfield left them facing a fourth down and nine.

Dud's punt was off the side of his foot. The ball sliced out of bounds at the Packer twenty-two. Dud sat on the bench, head down.

The Colt kicker never put his team in a hole that way, he thought. *Yeah, but he was the best kicker in the league last season! Any kid ought to improve in a year.*

"Cut it out. You foozled it; no excuse! You're falling back to your natural form. You're still just a dud!"

The tall boy sitting hunched next beside Dud on the bench jerked a sharp look at him. "What's that you're mumbling?" Eric asked.

Dud abruptly realized that he had been thinking aloud. "Nothing," he said. "Forget it!"

"Uh-huh." Eric nodded. "In Texas we never thought much of a guy bad-mouthing himself." He hesitated. Then his tone changed and he went on slowly. "I'm not very good at this.

"You changed my whole outlook on things. I owe you a lot. It's been good for me and it's been good for your Packers."

One side of Eric's mouth lifted in a crooked grin. He said, "I'm from Texas, see. Keep in mind that Texans have a reputation for bragging. Okay, but now I have to convince you that you have done more for the Packers than I have.

"Get it out of your nut that you're a dud! To-night you've been close to matching this best-kicker-in-the-league Colt. You have put points on the board for the Packers before, and I would bet you'll put some up there tonight!"

It was not that he didn't appreciate Eric's pep talk. Dud simply could not overlook the fact that the Colts had the ball well within the range of their kicker—and his poor punt was to blame.

The Colts went all out for a touchdown. They made a first down at the ten. Two tries into the line were stopped for a net gain of three yards. They tried a third down pass. No good.

Then the Colt kicker calmly lifted a field goal over the crossbar. Colts, 10; Packers, 6. The score was unchanged when the half ended. Dud Benton dragged slowly off the field. Whatever had made him think he deserved everybody's confidence?

CHAPTER THIRTEEN

Duds Sometimes Prove Live

DUD BENTON sat on the bench and stared out at the line of Packers stretched across the field for the second half kickoff. He was grateful for Coach Keefer's swat on the seat of the pants when the team was notified intermission was over. Okay, so Coach meant it telling me to keep my chin up, Dud thought. The score is still 10-6. I blew the PAT and foozled the punt that put them in position for the field goal.

He sat there and watched the Colts move the ball for five consecutive first downs after carrying the kickoff back to their twenty-eight. The Packer defense threw the Colt passer for a loss at the thirty. They completed a pass. Third down at the twenty. A line smash failed to make first down. The Colts lined up for a field goal try. The kick was good.

Colts, 13; Packers, 6.

Eric ran the kickoff to the twenty-nine. Going into the huddle, Dud clutched Eric's arm. "You've got to take us to a touchdown," Dud said. "You've *got* to!"

Eric made no promise. But in a sustained drive, the boy from Texas had never called plays more brilliantly. He mixed passes, keepers, off-tackle smashes by Klock, a sweep by Howell and then a reverse for a fourth straight down at the Colt twelve.

"We'll pass," he said in the huddle. "Maybe short, maybe into the end zone. You receivers get open. Keep those guys off my neck, you blockers! Hut!"

Eric took Dimarzio's handback, hid the ball behind his hip. But not too well. He wanted the defense to see it. A linebacker yelled, "Watch it! He's faking a pass! He's going to run!"

Eric suddenly swerved three strides back. The Colt secondary was caught following what they thought was the flow of the play to the right. Eric fired a "clothes-line pass" to the left. Whitey Howell stood all alone at the three. He caught the ball and scampered into the end zone.

"Nothing to it!" Eric nodded as he walked beside Dud to mark the spot he would set the ball for

Dud's try for the PAT. "Stand back there and do all the things Keefer told you to do!"

Dud's kick was as near perfect as a place kick could have been. Figures on the scoreboard changed to Packers, 13; Colts, 13.

Nobody could have denied that the Colt return of the next kickoff was a brilliant individual effort. Their boy playing deep fumbled the ball. Recovering, he dodged the first wave of tacklers, reversed his field, dodged two more tackle tries, and was finally run out of bounds at the Packer thirty.

An aroused defense held three Colt plays to a four yard advance. It was fourth down at the twenty-six, but the way the Colt kicker whammed the football it might as well have been from the six. The ball cleared the crossbar by five feet.

Colts, 16; Packers, 13.

"We can beat this team," Coach Keefer told his offense unit before they went out to receive the kickoff. "Let's go!"

Then Whitey Howell fumbled the kickoff.

A Colt recovered the fumble at the eleven. The defense dug in. Three crashing line efforts netted the Colts a scant four yards gained. But their kicker booted from the fourteen and the score was Colts, 19; Packers, 13. One minute left to play in the third quarter.

Thirteen points put on the scoreboard in seven minutes. The remaining sixty seconds and five minutes and four seconds of the fourth period passed before another scoring threat developed.

Al Dimarzio roared down under a punt and hit the receiver squarely at the twenty-two. The hard tackle jolted the ball from the Colt's grasp. Players dove at the loose ball. It squirted from beneath a Colt, a Packer, another Colt before Dimarzio fell on the oval and snuggled it close.

Packer ball, first down at the twenty. Dick Klock plunged for barely a yard. Linemen and one linebacker rushed Eric so hard that he threw a hurried pass short of Paul Field. Then the Colts smelled out a quarterback-draw and banged Eric down for a loss back to the twenty. A boy ran out from the Packer bench to replace a lineman.

"Go for a field goal," he told Eric. "Coach's orders. Then we get possession of the ball with a short kickoff and ram that thing into scoring position again!"

"It's farther than I've ever kicked one!" Dud protested. "Migosh! It's farther than their guy's record kick!"

"So you'll break his record," Eric said calmly. "You've booted 'em enough above the bar to carry more than twenty-seven yards. Get all the foot you've got into this one. Hold 'em off, you guys!"

Dud kept his head down and met the ball solidly and squarely. His teammates kept rushers from breaking through long enough to take away any chance of blocking the kick. The ball rose beautifully, dropped over the crossbar with feet to spare.

But the referee did not signal a score. Instead he called the Colt captain to him. Whitey Howell had literally held off a Colt lineman. The long field goal did not count.

"I didn't get a good blocking angle on him," Whitey moaned. "I grabbed him before I really thought!"

The holding penalty was fifteen yards. It looked as though the Packer scoring chance was gone; the game was lost. Dud Benton could not kick a field goal from beyond the forty yard line. The Packers would have to punt.

"I've got a hunch we can turn this into a good break," Eric said. He called for timeout and ran to the sideline. He talked earnestly with Coach Keefer. Eric's tone was charged with suppressed excitement when he came into the huddle.

"Coach bought my hunch," he said. "We're going to pull a fake punt! Dimarzio snaps to Dud in the deep spot. Dud, you start to swing your leg then act confused and run to the left. I'll be on that side like I'm blocking for a kick. You slip me the ball and tear on downfield to block. Howell, Field and Burch run pass routes. I'll hit whoever is open. We're going all the way. Hut!"

The snap was just a little high. By the time Dud pulled the ball in, a huge lineman was lunging at him. Dud did not have to put on an act—he was really confused. A dud ought not to be expected to play an important part in a made-up-out-here trick play!

He had never been more relieved than when he handed the ball to Eric. He raced downfield, ready to block a Colt.

Eric scanned the field while he scrambled away from a potential tackler. Colt defenders had reacted quickly. Howell was well covered. A defensive back ran stride for stride with Burch. Paul Field had his man beaten, was slanting out. Just as Eric was about to throw, Field cut sharply—and slipped. He stumbled three strides then sprawled to the ground.

The Colt Eric had scrambled away from pursued him, and threw his bulk at the Packer quarterback. Eric yelled, "Dud! Grab this thing!"

He threw while being tackled, barely got the ball away, but it bored through the air straight at Dud.

Dud Benton had never caught a pass in a game. He bobbled the ball. He half-stumbled four strides before he had it firmly clutched against his chest. The goal posts looked at least the length of the field away.

The defensive back covering Whitey Howell almost caught Dud from behind at the five. But when the Colt reacted and dashed after Dud, Whitey out-raced the defensive back and threw a great

block. The threat was wiped out and Dud rumbled on into the end zone.

Teammates mobbed him. They jumped on him and each other. After the referee placed the ball at the try-for-point line, Eric grabbed Dud's arm. "Kick this point and we've got 'em!" he said. "Our defense will hold onto the lead!"

Dud nodded. He felt numb but determined. He had kicked better PAT's—the ball wobbled over the bar barely missing the left upright. But it DID miss.

Packers, 20; Colts, 19.

The defense unit made sure that potential deep pass receivers were well-covered. They gave short yardage, but kept ballcarriers from going wide. The Colts tried a long pass with less than ten seconds to play—and Manny Dillon intercepted. Eric crouched, called off a string of meaningless numbers, took the handback and fell to the ground. He lay there while time ran out.

Coach Keefer had one arm around Dudley Benton and the other around Eric Rogel as the Packers came off the field. "Hunches pay off sometimes," the coach said. He chuckled and his eyes twinkled. "Duds sometimes prove to be live, too!"

"Am I ever glad this one exploded! Wowie!" Whitey Howell whooped, whacked Dud. "That block of mine kind of made up for the penalty that cost us the swell field goal you kicked!"

"What really counts most is that we're First Half champs," Eric said. "Now, we'll go after the Second Half—and be the first outfit to play an All Star team."

Eric grinned at Dudley Benton. "We'll make another deal," he said. "I'll work on coming up with hunches; you keep your fuse lit, ready to explode—Dud!"